ECHO HILL
By
W.H. BESWICK

Paranormal Research is not something to be taken lightly. Nor is it a game or the subject of a reality show, especially if you plan on going to Echo Hill. This is a quote from the mother of a son who went to Echo Hill Hill and vanished. His case is still open.

PROLOGUE

"We should have never come here," Walt said more to himself than the young woman beside him. They both huddled under a tree. The low boughs offered some protection from the pouring rain. The twenty-nine-year-old man had been born and raised in California, where it rained but nothing like this. This was a cold, hard rain that drenched their supposed waterproof jackets. He could feel the water inside his boots soaking his socks. The cold sent shivers through his body. Shivers that he was sure was freezing his very soul. He miserably stared into the darkness with his hands crossed his chest in a feeble attempt to get warmth. When there was no response to his statement, he glanced at the young woman beside him. Her hood was pulled down, covering her face, but like him, she shivered, not only from the cold and rain.

Colleen had never been a believer in God, but now, right, she was praying to the deity she had mocked her entire life. Fear was a great motivator when it came to believing in God. Walt said something, but she ignored his remark. She was focused on the trees that surrounded her. Just a day ago, in the sunlight, she had marveled at the beauty of this place. Tall majestic trees that reached up into the blue sky. Their leaf-filled branches spread out in what she thought was a welcoming gesture. Now, they looked more like the shadow monsters she had feared as a child. The branches now have long, sharp claws reaching for you. The wind sounded more like a growl or moan of something evil. You just turned on the light, and the monsters were gone.

There was no light here.

Was there ever?

The hike had been fun, laughter, joking about their pains from the steep winding trail—the joy of seeing a deer with their fawns. A family of raccoons scurrying away but then turning to look back with those cute masked faces. Sitting around the campfire and seriously discussing why they were there. In her mind, she never expected they would find anything. She was not a believer in ghosts, but she was in love. Twenty-three and deeply in love.

Now, she was a believer in God and ghosts.

Now, she just wanted to go home. Home where it was warm and dry. Home where there were no ghosts or evil witches. A chill ran through her body, but it wasn't from the rain or cold. She turned and saw the same look of fear in Walt's face.

He had heard it, too...maybe he felt it.

"Oh God, she is coming," Walt said with a whimper. He glanced at the young blonde woman beside him. It was his fault they were here. He moved in front of her and threw out his arms. "LEAVE HER ALONE! TAKE ME!"

"PLEASE! WE JUST WANT HO HOME!" Colleen sobbed.

They both saw the black shape move toward them. They both screamed.

PART 1
CHAPTER 1

THE REALITY SHOW STAR

"Audrey, do you find that being the daughter of one the richest men in America is a handicap or benefit in your paranormal research?"

"First off. I have my own money. I don't need my father's support for my research. Obviously, having money is a definite advantage. I can buy the best equipment and hire the best people. What is annoying me? Do people need to take my research seriously? What can the daughter of a billionaire be interested in regarding the paranormal? I do have a degree. Granted, it is in the cinema, but I graduated at the top of my class. Considering how competitive film school is. That is no small feat. If you check with my family and friends, I have always been interested in the paranormal. I had my first encounter with a ghost when I was ten."

"Your show does have high ratings, but many critics point out that your father buys a lot of commercial time for your show. Plus, you are a beautiful woman, and some of the outfits you wear on your show..."

"Stop right there. Do I go into these haunted places wearing a mini-shirt and stiletto boots? No, I wear whatever outfit is practical. As for my father, I am supposed to be mocked because I look good in jeans or shorts. If you knew my father, he wouldn't have spent money lightly. Trust me, if he wasn't making money off my show. He wouldn't be buying airtime. Once again, I have my own money."

"Another criticism is you go to what many people consider safe places..."

"Safe places? That's just some whiners who don't have the guts to go out and do what I do. Do you consider Echo Hill a safe place?"

"You are going to Echo Hill...no one goes to Echo Hill anymore...."

"No one but me."

CHAPTER 2

THAT WOULD BE NO

"No one goes up to Echo Hill, young lady."

"We have permission." Audrey Lang said with a smile.

"Now, Miss Lang, don't go lying to me." Sheriff Adam Royal said with a small smile. He looked across the battered desk belonging to his father and grandfather. Now, it was his desk and the badge on his chest. Most times, it was a straightforward job, but today it was annoying. His grey eyes took in the young woman sitting across from him. He had seen her on TV. More than once. Being the daughter of a billionaire was expected, especially when she looked like one of those Victoria's Secret models.

She was indeed quite beautiful. Her cheekbones, chin, and eyes gave her a face that he was sure came from God or some very talented doctor. But those green eyes were all hers. Sparkling with...

With what?

The black leather jacket with a matching skirt and red blouse was probably from Rodeo Drive or some store back in New York. Adam wouldn't know. He noticed the two top buttons of her bright blouse were undone. Giving the world a hint of her bosom. Adam was too much in love with his younger wife to be bothered. The wife who shopped at Fred Meyers or Target. She was always thrilled when she found a bargain.

The sheriff noted Miss Lang's long red curls fell from her face in a beautiful but unnatural way. It reached all the way down her back. It was cut into a straight, perfect line above her slender waist. He wondered why the only daughter of one the wealthiest men in the world works. Let alone hosting such a ridiculous show.

Then he reminded himself why she was here.

Maybe not that ridiculous.

"Fine, I really don't need permission. It is public land." Audrey said with a tone that reminded this small-town sheriff who she was. The twenty-four-year-old eyed the man sitting behind the small wooden desk in the small office. A small man in a small office in a big world. His well-pressed uniform shirt was tan with patches on the side. A silver badge was pinned to the front pocket. He looked in his forties, but his hair was still coal black, and the only wrinkles on his face were around his eyes.

Laugh lines.

For some reason, his friendly attitude and tone of voice annoyed her. Most people treated her with more respect...even fear. Not this tiny man. He showed no hint of fear or even respect. He was amused. She felt her face blush when that smug smile came to his lips.

"I thought you did your homework?" Adam said. Boy, that was the lovely perfume she was wearing. His wife probably knew what that scent was. It smelled expensive. Everything about this young lady screamed wealth and power. But that was out in the real world. Not here. Here, Miss Audrey Lang was just another annoyance. "Three years back, the town sold Echo Hill. It is now private property. I know the owners and they didn't give you permission. The reason I know this is because right after the sale was done. The owners tore down the only bridge that ran up the old logging road. Farther up, there was a log that you could use to cross a deep creek. That was cut up for firewood. Then, they planted bamboo trees along the path. My god, that stuff grows fast. Along with that, he planted these bushes that had the biggest damn thorns I ever saw. They have made it clear they don't want anyone up there. I don't want anyone up. So you are not going up there."

"Are you telling me there is no trail anymore? No way to get up there."

"Well, if you were really determined. But carrying cameras and other equipment would make it quite difficult."

"That's my problem. I promised my viewers the most haunted place in this part of the country."

"It's not a problem for you because you ain't going. Do you know how many times my father and his father went up that hill? Too many to count. People got hurt going up there looking for the fools who wanted to see Echo Hill. Everyone who has gone up there looking for Echo Hacker has died or just vanished."

"Not everyone. Two people came back."

"Yes, two people came back," he said, leaning back in his chair and glancing back as it creaked. Guess who owns Echo Hill now?"

CHAPTER 3

MONEY TALKS

Audrey came out of the same sheriff's office, looking annoyed. She pulled her phone out of her purse, matching her shoes perfectly. Her driver was a young man hired for the day because he knew the fastest way to get this nothing-little town back in the hills of Oregon. He could see the anger and stepped back, giving the young lady plenty of room. As she rushed past, he turned away, not wanting to be caught looking at his employer. It was almost impossible. That leather skirt is so tight and short. He forced himself to look up at the tall tree covering the mountain instead of looking at what he really wanted to look at. A light fog lingered over the tops of the trees. It looked pretty beautiful. It didn't look like the kind of place ghosts would hang out.

But what did he know?

Audrey was fuming. She was used to people not only being afraid of her but respecting the power she represented. She spoke, and they obeyed. Then, his small-town sheriff rocked back and forth in his chair with that arrogant grin. She usually called someone to complain about this small town in Oregon, but what could anyone do. This is the first time anyone here has worked for any of the father's companies. No one she could think of knew about this dot on the map. All the local businesses were family-owned.

Local businesses. That was a joke.

There was a gas station, a small store, a diner, and a sporting goods store, and that was it.

The local mayor and sheriff seemed too honest. She could see that. So, money hadn't been offered. She hit speed dial. Before the person on the other end of the call could say a word, she yelled, "What the hell! I thought you did the research on this place."

"I did, Miss Lang."

"Then how did you miss that Echo Hill is now privately owned? Tell me, Jerry. How did you miss that?"

"Huh?" Jerry said. "Maybe they did the deal face to face, not using the Internet, signing actual papers. Okay, okay, it's got to be registered somewhere. I'll find the owners."

"I already know who the owners are. There are the only two people who went up Echo Hill and came back."

"You mean those two? Who would have thought writing horror novels could make you such big bucks."

"Oh God, have you never heard of Stephen King?" Audrey groaned. "Find them. I'll make them an offer they can't refuse."

"Very Godfather."

Audrey just clicked off. She angrily looked up at the mountain known as Echo Hill—so close yet so far.

"Those two writers aren't let you set foot on that mountain."

The tall blonde turned and stared at the small, skinny man. He was wearing old faded jeans patched with red cloth in several places. His shirt was red flannel that looked new. The man couldn't been more than twenty, but his face showed he had a hard life, or maybe he just drank. A day-old beard covered the chin of his oval face. A beat-up trucker's cap rested on a head with hair cropped very short. His blue eyes were bright. When he smiled. Audrey expected to see some missing teeth, but they were all there and white.

"The town let them have Echo Hill cheap. Every time someone died or vanished up there. Someone would try to sue the town. Like there is any money here. It still costs them money to defend themselves. So you see, the town and those writers had the same goal. Stop anyone from going up there to stop the lawsuits. Well, I think the writers actually believe in ghosts."

Audrey studied the man. He was definitely not college-educated, but he was brilliant in his own way. She stepped closer. "Have you been up there?"

"Just to what is left of the logging camp...the place you want to go is a little further up. My brother got the shakes, so we came back down."

"You know a way up there."

"I do. I should tell you. It will be a hard hike. Have to cross a couple of creeks and such. Harder if you are carrying heavy gear. You are going up to film for your TV show." He said, moving closer to get a better look at the redhead. His brother says she looked so good on TV because of lighting and makeup. His brother was wrong about that.

"But you can get me up there." She said, feeling the man's eyes leer over her. She was used to it. They could all look, but no touching was allowed. Wouldn't the world be shocked to discover Audrey Lang was a virgin? According to the media, she had dozens of lovers. Now, that was fake news.

"That depends on what you are willing to pay. Like I said, my brother got the shakes. He is better in the woods than I am. But for the right price, he might be persuaded..."

Audrey smiled. Now, they were in her ballpark. Money.

CHAPTER 4

GHOSTS PAY THE BILLS

Professor Richard Wolsky walked into his classroom. It was packed. It was always packed on the day he discussed Echo Hill. The most haunted place in Oregon. In the top ten for the entire nation. He understood the fascination. It had all the correct elements. A beautiful woman was wronged. Evil, greedy men. And over the last two hundred years, almost a hundred people have died or gone missing. No matter how many times he told the story. The room was packed. His eyes drifted over the room. Usual crowd. The students that were actually registered for the class. The rest were a mixture of old and young. I am here for the ghost story. He spotted the short blonde girl sitting in front again. How many times had she been here? Last time, there had been a tall girl with a mass of angry red hair with her. Her friend looked amused at the story during the whole lecture. This made him like the young lady. She wasn't taken in by his story.

The tall, lean man walked to the podium. His jacket was dull white, while his shirt and slacks were black, as was his hair. Many thought a little too black. It was combed back with gel, making him look like a modern-day greaser from the fifties. It was the only way he could cover up the growing bald spot. He would have to look into another way to deal with that someday, but he still needs to. Around his neck was a gold chain with a round medallion and an eye in the center. He told people it was the all-seeing eye. It gave him powerful protection.

Which in his line of study was very important.

Professor Wolsky was in his mid-forties but could pass for much younger thanks to good genes and the lack of sun in Oregon. A bright sun will cause wrinkles. There were very few signs of his age on his face. Black framed glasses that he didn't need resting on his hook nose. Another prop for the image.

Wolsky had no notes; he didn't need any. He knew the story by heart. He had also covered it in his last book, a best seller. This made him smile. Thanks to his books, he was considered one of the nation's top experts on the paranormal when it came to ghosts.

Not demons. Ghosts.

He was very clear on that.

Richard always pointed out that ghosts and demons were completely different creatures. Demons had never been human and were always evil, while ghosts had been people and weren't always evil.

His interest in the paranormal had come late in life. It had all started when he heard rumors they were going to make cuts in his department. He was in the English Department of Oregon Tech. Something told him his creative writing classes would probably be on the block. Back then, he was in his mid-thirties, and finding another college position would be next to impossible with degrees in English Lit and Mythology. The hard reality was he just needed to publish more. That moron Deswick was already into the fifth book of his young adult series. They were very popular, so he was safe.

A teenager fighting aliens.

Stupid.

On the other hand, Deswick was driving a Lexus.

The professor had been worried, but one night, he watched a reality show about ghost hunting. It made him laugh at the foolishness of it all. What qualifies one to hunt ghosts? It was followed by another one. And another. And another. That night, he had an inspiration that would change his life.

Over the weekend, he did some quick research and compiled a proposal for a new class: GHOSTS: FACT AND FICTION. He pitched the idea to the department head, who laughed but then said he would let him teach the class over the summer if he also taught a whole summer of basic grammar classes.

Wolsky agreed.

No one was more surprised than him when the class filled up on one day. Getting subject material for the class was a breeze. He watched the Ghost Hunter shows now, taking notes, Googled a lot of information, and even watched some horror movies.

Some people wanted to enroll in the class on the first day of class even though it was packed. He was terrified on the first day. Stumbling to the podium and then looking out at those eager faces. Suddenly, all his notes seemed foolish. A hot sweat drenched his shirt. It was too late to back out. He plowed ahead with the class. Once again, he was shocked when at the end of the class. Several people had clapped for him. In the next class, he stepped up his game with visual aids. This was a hit. By the end of the summer, he decided to put his degree to work. He found several haunted places in the country and wrote about them. He visited several of them but mainly googled or gleamed information from the reality shows. The book took little time to write.

Two things happened over the next year: the book was published, and four classes on the Paranormal were approved. By the end of the year, his book was a best seller. His publisher was asking for another, which was in the works. The last two things were that he was made head of the new Paranormal Studies Department.

Department.

What a joke.

It was him and two other teachers. One was an actual ghost hunter that had turned out to be very handy.

But most important. Richard was also given tenure.

With his job secure and the money coming in from his book. Life was good.

The professor was amazed. Ghosts. Who would think? Ghosts had saved his career. And he didn't even believe in them.

Professor Richard Wolsky looked over the class and said, "So, let's talk about Echo Hill."

CHAPTER 5

ECHO HACKER

"The Echo Hill Witch," Wolsky said with outstretched hands. He let these words hang in the air for a moment. "There very few people who haven't heard of Echo Hill...actually, I think it is closer to a mountain than a hill, but that's not what we are here to discuss."

There were the expected chuckles. Wolsky smiled and knew he had them.

"We are here to talk about Echo Hacker. The supposed Echo Hill Witch..."

The professor scanned the room. As always, there were some confused looks.

Good.

"Echo Hacker doesn't fit the stereotypical image of a witch. According to journals and other sources, she was only in her twenties and beautiful with blonde hair. The fact is there are no records of her casting spells, cursing anyone, or abducting children. I hate to disappoint you. But Echo was no Blair Witch."

Almost everyone leaned forward. The class wanted more.

"The word witch didn't become associated with her name until long after her death. Well, not only her death but many more deaths, including the man who...well, started it."

"So she wasn't a witch?" A young man in the front row asked.

"Not in the traditional sense. Echo did live back in the woods all by herself. It is known she knew a great many herbal remedies. Helped a lot of people. From all accounts, she appeared to be a good person. But we are getting ahead of ourselves. Let's talk about the first time Echo Hacker's name came up. The date is debated, but Echo Hacker's name came up sometime between 1840 and 1845..."

"Did she really just appear?' A young brunette asked.

"There some who say she appeared in a puff of smoke. I have my doubts. We know for certain when the first wagon train pulled into the place now known as Echo Hill. The young woman was already there. According to legend, Echo stood in a field as if waiting for them. Think about that beautiful blonde woman standing in the middle of nowhere. No one else. No family. No other settlers. The wagon master had questions, but Echo ignored them. She simply said. "I understand so of your people are sick. I may be able to help them."

"The fact was there were quite a few sick. Echo tended to all of them. She stayed with them long to make sure anyone was well. She took no pay but had only one request. Her exact words if you believe the records."

Once again, the professor paused, as he always does at this point in the narrative. Then, with a chilled tone, he said, "Do as you will with the surrounding land, but stay off the hill. The hill is mine."

Richard let the words sink in. They always had the desired effect, even though most had heard them. They had been quoted numerous times in TV shows and specials. To many, this was the only warning that Echo gave.

"At first, her request was accepted. You can't farm or raise cattle on a mountain. There were plenty of other trees in the area to cut down. And the young woman had just saved their lives. The newcomers didn't see much of Echo. In time, they discovered a small family graveyard close to her home. So she hadn't come out alone. That took away some of the mystery of the young lady. She stayed on her mountain but would only come to the small town when she needed supplies or to tend to the sick. This arrangement went on for years."

At this moment, he paused and put an image of a beautiful blonde woman on the screen. It wasn't a real picture of Echo. It was the picture of the actress who played Echo in a TV special. It didn't matter. It got the attention of his class.

"There were questions. Where did Echo come from? Why did she stay up there on the hill all by herself? Her family had all passed away. A young woman living by herself didn't seem right. But the big question for the women was why Echo never seemed to grow old. No grey hair or wrinkles appeared on her face. These things led to gossip, but nothing bad. It certainly didn't stop the young men from trying to court the young lady. The town grew, but the agreement was kept."

That was when Harry Johnson showed up.

CHAPTER 6

THE END OF ECHO HACKER

"So, depending on what books you read or TV shows you have watched or even Googled, a small group of people paint Harry Johnson as the victim," Richard said, almost with a snort.

"It is my opinion that Harry Johnson is the real villain in this story," Wolsky said with a grin. "Without Harry, there would be no Echo Hill. Everyone, including Echo, was happy, living in peace. As far as most of the settlers were concerned, there was no reason to go up Echo Hill as it was now known. Yes, you had to hike a little farther for trees to build a house or barn, but Echo had no problem with someone going onto her hill to collect fallen branches for a fire or even hunt game. But her trees and plants could not be touched."

The professor moved out from behind the podium and closer to the class. "What do we know about Harry Johnson? The one fact you have to know is. Mr. Johnson wasn't rich but destitute, but the stories about his wealth are false. We know he was young and handsome. Most important, Harry was arrogant. He was one of those people who was used to getting his way. He came from Boston. Ending up in Echo Hill. Not by choice. Apparently, he had debts and had impregnated with three young ladies. Debts and deflowering young ladies were unacceptable behavior at the time. You could end up in prison or worse if the young lady had male relatives who objected to Harry's actions. So Harry left the East to seek his fortune and probably to save his neck."

This always produced some chuckles. Richard smiled and nodded at his own joke.

"You have a man with dubious character come to this small town. A man who is obviously used to having his way with the young ladies. According to my research."

You had to love Google.

"The moment Harry saw Echo, he wanted her. I am sure it wasn't love or not completely about lust. I would like to think he was like Gaston from that movie. An arrogant man used to having women almost swoon when he gave them some attention. Needless to say, Echo rebuffed all his advances. Now, I will be honest with you. The events that followed could be clearer and more specific. These are the facts. Harry started rumors about the strange lady on the mountain."

Wolsky wandered among his students and stared at a young lady using her phone. She looked up, blushed, and put away the phone.

"Peer pressure and gossip, as we all know, has caused more damage to people's lives than anything else. People love to gossip. As long as it is not about them. One night, Harry and several other men. It has been confirmed that the liquor flowed freely in the local tavern. These men went up Echo Hill. There really is no record of what happened, but the bottom line is that Echo was dead by morning. That same morning, now sober, they realized what they had done. In a feeble attempt to cover up their crime. They buried her not in the small family graveyard but in the woods under a pile of stones."

Professor Wolsky spread out his hands as he took in the class. Then he clapped them together with a loud crack. He walked back to the front of the classroom. "These murderers went back to town and were never held accountable for their crimes. Harry Johnson even moved into Echo's home and started to cut down her beloved trees. Well, to be honest, not many trees were actually cut down. The townspeople may have looked the other way. Apparently, Echo held a grudge. I am going to read to you from the journal of Albert Smith. He worked for Harry Johnson."

The professor returned to his podium and tapped a key on his laptop. "There is no date, so we don't know how much time has passed since Echo's murder. Ah, here we are."

CHAPTER 7

FIRST BLOOD

I am the last one. Everyone is dead. Well, maybe not that asshole, Harry. The last time I saw him, he was running like a fool. He was in the woods, screaming he was going home. I don't think he is going to make it.

Why should he? He started this mess.

Hell, I wasn't even there. All those fools are dead except for Harry. I just came up here to chop down some trees.

We should have left after the first accident.

Accident? I am still lying to myself.

We are cutting down this big pine. We made the cut so it would fall to the left. It should have fallen to the left. It fell to the right. Landed right on top of George and the kid. Squashed them like a couple bugs. I saw it fall. It was like someone gave that big tree a big shove.

Told ourselves it was bad luck.

It was terrible luck that Tommy missed his swing with his axe. Chopped off his leg from the knee down. I had never seen anything like that. Tommy screamed, trying to use his hands to stop the blood from spurting out his leg. It was like a goddamn geyser. We all just stood there. It was like something was holding us in place. We just watched Tommy bleed to death. Crying and begging for help. We did nothing.

Still, that wasn't enough.

You know why we stayed. Harry showed us some gold nuggets he found in the woman's house. Not small pebbles. Stones. He was holding a small fortune in the palm of his hand. Still, more was needed for most of the boys. They all took off. It was just me, Teddy, Elmer, and Harry.

We forgot about the trees and started looking for gold.

How stupid was that? Not one of us knew a thing about finding gold. It's not like you can see gold nuggets lying on the ground. They are a bunch of fools wandering around looking for gold.

It didn't matter. We never got the chance. Teddy got mauled to death by a bear. The biggest blackest damn bear I ever saw. It wasn't just the size but its eyes. Its eyes were red. Not blood red, but the red you see in a fire. Elmer, who was there that night, ran off. I followed him. He came to a pile of stones and started pulling them away like a crazy man. He begged her to forgive him and sobbed like a baby. Harry came up beside me and watched for a second. Then he stepped forward, yelling for Elmer to stop.

It was then I realized this was the witch's grave.

Now, whoever is reading this won't believe it, but sure, as there is a god. It happens. An arm covered with mud and blood came right out of that pile of stones. It grabbed Elmer around the neck and pulled him down into the grave. Kicking and screaming, he was, but it did no good. That hand pulled Elmer right down into the grave. The screaming stopped. Then, the rocks all rolled back in place. I just stood there and watched. Rocks moving all by themselves. Soon, the grave looked like it had never been touched. Then the blood came. It began to seep out between the stones. It looks black as the night under the moonlight.

That was when Harry decided he had enough and ran off.

Now, I am sitting in the bunkhouse writing this. I tried to follow the road we had cut down to the town but kept ending up here. It's like the road we cut is just one big circle. The sun should be up by now, but it isn't. So I just started writing and waiting. There is no point in running.

I must have fallen asleep. The sun is up. I started laughing until I saw the words written on the wall. It sure looks like blood. The words are THIS IS MY HILL.

CHAPTER 8

GHOST HUNTER?

"This was the last entry in the journal." The professor said, looking up. "But it is not the last we heard of Albert. He managed to get back to town and told everyone what happened. According to legend, Albert left town using the few gold nuggets he found in his pants pocket. Search parties were sent up to the logging camp and Echo's house. They found the warning on the wall. It was blood. The bodies of some of the men who died were found. Harry and Elmer's bodies were never found. In a short time, sickness ran through the whole town. Almost everyone died. Those who didn't. Left."

"Sir, the town of Echo Hill is still there." An older man said.

"Have you been to Echo Hill?" Richard said, almost laughing. "It really isn't much of a town. More importantly, it is not built in the same spot. The original Echo Hill was on the North side of the mountain. The one you know is in the South. I have been there. Not one of the locals has set foot on Echo Hill."

Wolsky smiled like a man who knew what they were thinking.

"There were attempts to repopulate the town but failed. There were more than a few attempts to harvest the trees or look for the supposed gold up there, but all resulted in injury, death, or people just disappearing. The fact that Echo Hill is off the beaten path only adds to the legend. I am told that the logging industry says harvesting the trees just wouldn't be profitable. That is a good as reason as any."

This produced nervous chuckles.

Back in his office, Professor Wolsky leaned back in his chair and was deciding where to eat lunch when his phone beeped. He frowned after looking at the face. It was the president of the university. A shiver of fear ran down his spine, making the professor slightly nervous. The president had made no secret of what he thought of Wolsky, his classes, and books. But he brought in money, and that was all that mattered.

He tapped the face of his phone. "President Wilson, how can I help you?"

"I have some good news," the man on the phone said smugly. He could feel the man's smile when he said, "You may have the chance to visit Echo Hill."

"What...I mean, sir. No one goes to Echo Hill? It is private property. I have tried in the past..."

"You may have the chance to go now."

Richard's whole body slumped. He felt his face not only fall but turn white. A hot sweat drenched his body. For a second, he couldn't speak. Then managed to croak. "I don't understand."

"This will be good for the university and you. Details are still being worked out, but I suggest you pack your ghost-hunting gear."

The phone clicked off. The professor just sat there thinking. There had to be a way out of this. Echo Hill was the last place on Earth he wanted to go.

CHAPTER 9

BAD NEWS

The treadmill was great. So simple. Just one foot in front of the other. You could walk or run as slow or fast as you like. You could listen to music or watch TV. The runner did none of these. Just ran in place with her eyes closed. Shutting out the rest of the gym. The hot sweat that began to run down her burning flesh made her feel alive. The pounding heart in her chest added to this.

On the treadmill, she felt alive. This was important to her.

She listened to the rhythmic pounding of her expensive shoes on the moving rubber. It was like having someone beat a drum to help her keep her pace. Images of sweaty men rowing harder and faster sometimes filled her mind; other times, her mind was blank.

Not today. The young woman's mind was far from blank.

She was not thinking about the errands she had to run. There were none. Or chores around the house. The maid took care of those. What to make for dinner. She couldn't cook except for making coffee and P&J when needed. Now Walt could cook and even liked doing it. She could have thought of work in the traditional sense of the word. There was no clock to punch. No boss hovering over her shoulder. No quotas except the ones she set for herself.

What was her mind filled with it?

Her mind was usually filled with goblins, ghouls, vampires, werewolves, and other creatures of the night. It depended on whatever monster in her latest novel. Today was about a man returning to a small town that vampires had taken over. It was a sequel to one of her other books that had been compared to King's Salem's LOT. Like King had ownership of vampires in small towns? It didn't really matter to the runner. What matter was? Did the book sell? It did. So well, a sequel was almost demanded. Besides, it was easy money. Money was important to her. Not in the way it was important to others. The apartment she shared with her husband was small, with three bedrooms, three baths, two dens, and a family room. It was furnished more for comfort than style. Their cars were older. Their clothes had no designer labels. The maid was really their only luxury. There were occasional trips to places with hot sun, white beaches, and colorful drinks. But one needed those when their books took you to dark and creepy places.

The new book was already mapped out. The characters are created and ready to rumble, as they would say. All that was left was to think up nasty and exciting ways to kill vampires. The vampires were locked into the sucking blood thing. So, killing the vampires was the creative part. Yes, some would be staked. Others were forced into the sunlight. But that wasn't enough. Her writing partner and husband came up with the idea that would make it possible to kill vampires in new and different ways. His idea was. It wasn't the wood stake that killed the vampire but the faith behind it. You had faith that a wood stake would kill a vampire, and it did. The hero would learn to use his faith to use other weapons.

Guns. Knives. Any weapon suddenly became a possibility.

In the last hour, she had worked on four very juicy deaths and was working on the fifth when her phone rang. Annoyed, she opened her eyes. She recognized the caller and frowned. He knew not to disturb her while at the gym. The runner slowed the machine, tapped the face of her phone, and asked, "What?"

"We may have a problem."

"I am working on that..."

"It's about Echo Hill."

The runner punched the red stop button, grabbed the rails, and sighed. "What's the problem?"

CHAPTER 10

FIRST WARNING

Jerry Epstein was an atheist. He was also on probation. His computing skills had taken him to places the government had deemed illegal, unlike in the movies. It was only possible to cover some of your tracks. You always left tracks when you went onto the Net. He had been caught, convicted, and paroled. Unlike other hackers, Jerry had been lucky. He was allowed access to computers and the Internet. But it had been made clear. Next time, the cell door will be closed for a long time. The prison had actually scared Jerry straight.

No more hacking for him.

Unless it was ordered by his boss.

His boss was Audrey Lang. He did research for her show. It was simply called GHOSTS? The question mark was supposed to imply they were seeking the truth. What they were really seeking was the ratings. And the ratings were excellent, primarily because of Audrey. Not only was she hot, but whenever possible, she wore tight and somewhat revealing outfits. The fact she was the youngest daughter of one the wealthiest men in the world helped.

Jerry's job was finding and researching haunted places for Audrey to explore. He then did deeper research into whoever was involved to find anything Audrey or Carol could use to their advantage. The twenty-six-year-old had no interest in what they did with the information he sometimes dug up.

That wasn't his job.

The young man kept his distance between himself and Audrey. If the Feds came asking questions. He would throw the sexy redhead under the bus. A rich spoiled brat was better press than him. Jerry has no illusions about his relationship with Audrey. He is not handsome or ugly. The acne that plagued him in high school and college had cleared up but left scars. His John Lennon glasses actually fit his slender face.

His body had another issue. He had never gone to the gym and was addicted to Big Macs, Double Double burgers, fries, and strawberry milkshakes. Sitting in from of a computer all day had caused his butt and stomach to spread out. He was bottom-heavy. So, there was no chance in hell that Audrey would ever look in his direction except to give him an order or ask what he had found.

Jerry hit the keyboard and muttered a curse. He slumped back in his chair and glared at the three screens of his computer. This was impossible.

Carol Holtz looked sweet with her short, slender body and pixie haircut. The black curls streaked with green, wire-framed glasses and lips that always seem to be curved up into a grin. But spending five minutes with the twenty-four-year-old USC film school graduate, you realized there was nothing sweet about her. Her voice could be as cold as ice or hot as a flamethrower. Carol had no natural talent in writing, acting, or any of the technical aspects of filmmaking. However, she did have excellent organizational skills and drive. This made her a great producer. The young lady could have excelled in any corporation. Today, the movie business is where the money is, but more importantly, the world loves movie people. Carol wanted to be loved.

Carol had lucked out when she met Audrey Lang at USC. In her mind, Audrey was the cash cow every producer dreamed of having. She planted the seeds once she discovered her friend's interest in ghosts. One month after graduating, Carol started her own production company. She was technically Audrey's employee, but she ran the show. All Audrey had to do was look pretty in front of the camera, on the red carpet, and on the talk shows. The TV show had been a hit from the start. Since then, they have produced three horror movies that did very well. They would have done better if she had gotten Audrey to run around in a wet tee shirt or tight shorts while being chased by a mad killer, but no. At least she wore tight outfits for the show.

A lovely little film about a boy and his dog was making the rounds and getting some good press. The important thing was that Carol's name was being noticed by the bigger companies. She knew you couldn't hunt ghosts forever.

The young producer walked into the pigsty that Jerry called the office. His computer setup took up two tables: three monitors with keyboards and a mouse for each. Boxes of discarded computer parts and unopened boxes of electronic toys were piled along one wall. Three trash cans, all full, were pushed into a corner. More fast food and other papers were lying around the three cans.

Did the man eat nothing but burgers and fries?

"What you got?" Carol snapped, coming behind him, her eyes going over the three screens. One was the Google homepage. Another was the site on Echo Hill. The other was filled with what looked like gibberish to her but probably made sense to Jerry.

"I got nothing," Jerry said, whirling around. "I mean really nothing. I found basic stuff like where they were born, their relatives, where they went to school and old jobs. But after coming back from Echo Hill. Nothing. It's like they fell off the grid."

"They are best-seller authors," Carol growled, not liking what she heard. She was already nervous about Echo Hill. This was different from the other places they had gone. People had actually died. Gone missing. She didn't believe in ghosts or anything the show promoted, but something about this place wasn't right.

On top of that, they would have to sneak up there unless they tracked down the two owners and convinced them to let film. Audrey was already getting her team together. Some professor and psychic she had seen on TV.

"I know. It's bizarre." Jerry continued. "I have been to their website and other websites on them and their books. They all give basic information but no clue where they live. I can't even find any recent pictures of them. Walt and Colleen Wilkins are nowhere to be found. That's impossible."

"I assume you went to places most people can't go?" Carol said in a voice laced with ice.

"If you are talking about the IRS or any other federal agency. First, unlike TV and movies, getting in isn't easy. Plus, per our agreement. I don't go to those places."

"Fair enough," Carol said with a sigh. Her calm mind did some calculations. "So Echo Hill could be dangerous. That will get us the ratings. The Wilkins are rich but not as rich as our employer. Let them sue us. Pack your gear. We go leaving tomorrow."

"Carol." Jerry gasped. "Me. I am the research guy. I…"

"You actually know how to use those ghost-hunting tools. You'll see a nice bonus."

Before Jerry could answer, she turned and walked out of his office. There was never a goodbye. The young man slumped. Most times, he didn't mind going out in the field. He usually sat in a van, trailer, or room, watching the action on monitors.

Safe and sound.

But this time, they were hiking up a mountain. A mountain where people had died or vanished. He sighed deeply, turned back to his computer, and froze. The screens of all three monitors were now bright red. The keys of his keyboard began to click. The word stop appeared over and over, slowly filling the screen. Soon, the words started to appear faster and faster. Then, the fluorescent lights over his head began to flash. The door to his office slammed closed with a loud bang. His coffee mug flew up into the air and smashed against the wall. He watched the can of the coke he had just bought begin spinning around. It flew into the air. A second later, the dark liquid inside shot into the air like a geyser. Jerry doused in the sticky liquid. The three monitors are still red but are now flashing on and off. One word filled each screen.

DON'T GO THERE!

Jerry's chair rolled across the room with him still in it. It crashed against the door, sending him to the floor. He just lay there watching the screen flash over and over. The overhead lights exploded. Bright light filled the room before plunging the room into darkness. Shreds of glass came showering down on Jerry's head and body. Now, bright red monitors were the only light. It was like he was trapped in a neon hell. Finally, he managed to get to his knees. All three monitors exploded, sending another shower glass and sparks into the air. The door flew open.

Jerry crawled out of the room sobbing and ran.

CHAPTER 11

SECOND WARNING

Todd Vickers was just twenty-two and thrilled to have the job. It could have paid better, unlike most of his film school friends. He had a job with benefits. He got the job because his older brother knew his new boss. At first, he had assumed that Carol Holtz had been one of his brother's ex-girlfriends or lovers, but one meeting with the cold bitch had changed his mind. He decided that Carol needed to get laid or just drunk. She was a total control freak. His brother had warned him about this. Carol was worse.

Carol walked into the tech room. It was a large room lined with metal shelves. These same shelves were filled with cameras and all manner of electronic gear. There was a small metal desk with just a tiny chair. Both looked at Government Issues. Which they were. Carol had bought them off Craig's list. She knew where to cut corners. The camera and sound staff didn't need comfy offices. She watched the very tall man fiddle with his camera. Like all cameramen, he was dressed for comfort. Jeans, sneakers, and a Star Wars tee shirt. They never understood her obsession with those movies, but she did understand the money they made. Todd started to take down a heavy case to pack his gear. "No, we going to be hiking. You will have to put your gear in a backpack. You can find one down in supply. You have boots?"

"No," Todd said, looking down at his well-worn sneakers.

"I hope you are not planning on wearing those sneakers. We go up a mountain in Oregon. Get some boots and a heavy jacket. I need you at a hundred percent. You are the most important member of the team on this trip."

"What about Miss Lang?"

"Listen to me," Carol said coolly, moving closer to the young man. "There are no pictures of Echo Hill. No one has seen pictures of the logging camp or the witch's house. Understand. No video. No photos.

We will be the first. Even if we don't find any ghosts. The pictures and videos you take will be gold. So get the boots and jackets and most important. Don't screw up. You screw up, and it wouldn't be the ghosts you have to worry about."

A short, plump woman walked into the office. She glanced at the two people but showed no reason for interest. Maria Gonzalez had a round face with full lips and huge brown eyes. Her dark black was streaked with blonde. There was a ring on her nose. A hint of a tattoo peeked out from the short sleeve of her blouse. She went to shelves, took down a short pole, and fiddled with it. It clicked and extended out into a longer pole. She looked at Carol. "We are hiking, right?"

"Yes, you seen Jerry?" Carol asked.

"Nope. Problem?"

"His office a mess. He is not answering his phone. If he is not at the airport, his fat ass is fired. The flight is at eight. We check into a motel. Get a meal and get a good night's sleep. My plan is to get up the mountain. Get some videos and photos. Let Audrey do her thing, but I have no desire to spend the night up there. Understand. Do your jobs, and we will be home by Friday."

Carol nodded and walked out. Todd watched her walk out and then let out a sigh.

"She gives a hell of pep talk...Not." Maria said with a smile. "Relax. Yes, she is a bitch, but you do your job, and you will be fine."

"What happens to your old cameraman?" Todd asked, pulling the camera close to his chest.

"Ghost killed him. Very sad.

"What?"

Maria laughed. "Dude, you got to relax. No such thing as ghosts."

"But you work for this show?"

"I am the sound person. I am never in front of the camera, nor will you be. I don't believe in ghosts. But I believe in the paychecks and bonuses Carol gives out when she is happy with the show. Focus. This is Echo Hill. The big one. Take your pictures and videos. You're good. Plus, you will have a hell of a pickup line for the ladies."

"Hell, that's right. This job just got better."

A ticking sound made them both turn.

Three empty metal film reels were hanging on the wall. One reel was slowly turning, and then the second started to turn.

"If that last one starts, I am out of here," Carol said as she watched the two reels spin faster and faster.

The third began to spin. Soon, all three spun so fast that they looked like silver discs on the wall. They began to wobble.

"Watch out! Todd screamed, dropping to the floor and pulling Maria down with him.

The reels flew off the wall and went right over their heads. All three buried themselves in the opposite wall. Then overhead lights exploded, sending the room into darkness.

The two terrified people rolled over and stared at the reels. Then, they crawled out of the room. Carol walked up and looked down at them. "What the hell are you two doing?"

They both pointed to the room. Carol stepped in and looked around. The lights were on, and the reels were back on their hooks. There was no sign of any damage to the walls.

"Get up off the floor," she growled. We have to move. The owners might know what we are up to. Our departure time is no six. Move."

CHAPTER 12

THE REAL EXPERT

Alex Wagner rushed around his office, stuffing gear into a duffle bag. He was a tall, muscular man with close-cropped blonde hair. The work shirt and jeans looked old and worn. His office is small and cluttered with file boxes, books, and just messy piles of paper. One wall is covered with a map of the United States. Colorful pins are stuck all over the surface. Alex opens a drawer and takes out a small yellow handheld device. He clicks it on. Beeping fills the room.

Wolsky walked into the office and watched.

Alex takes a digital camera out of the same drawer and checks it. It then he notices Wolsky.

"You should be packing. We left two hours earlier." Alex said. Then looks into the professor's face. He pulls the man into the office and slams the door close. Then, he pushes Wolsky up against the door, grabbing the lapels of his jacket. "You do not wimp out on me. We are going to Echo Hill. Understand? This is huge. I am not going to miss out on this."

"Alex, you don't need me," Wolsky said.

"I know that, but the world doesn't. I know you are a fraud. I put up with you because you bring money into this department. I got to use that money to do some actual paranormal research. I don't mind sharing my findings with you. Because that means more money and more research. This could be the one that makes people stop laughing, sit up, and notice how important our work is. Oh, pardon me. My work. Now man up and get your gear."

"You can go…"

"Miss Lang asked for you. They want Professor Richard Wolsky, not Alex Wagner." Alex said, letting go of the jacket and almost politely dusting it off. "I will have your back. You already know how to use the EMF detector, so work with that. You do not see the big picture. It doesn't matter if we find anything. We just have to get to Echo Hill and get back. Then we are gold. More money. More research. I will not let my life's work go down the toilet because you can't find your balls."

"What if it is really haunted?" Wolsky asks, suddenly looking less afraid.

"I prove some of my theories, and you will become even more famous. And richer."

"You got my back?"

"Always. Your gear is down in the car, right?"

"Yes," Wolsky said in a defeated tone.

"My man! Now, let's go hunt some ghosts."

Alex's duffle beeps loudly. He walks over and looks inside. The EMF detector is beeping. He takes it out and smiles. "Excellent."

"What does that mean?" Wolsky asked.

"It is either broken, or someone is warning us to stay away from Echo Hill."

"Who?"

"A ghost, you silly boy. It just got so much better."

Richard doesn't share his friend's enthusiasm. He nervously strokes his chin.

CHAPTER 13

POVERTY MAKES YOU DESPERATE

"You shouldn't have taken the job," Heath growled, sounding more like an animal. He was a big man standing well over six feet with a broad body that appeared to not have an ounce of fat. His curly blond hair falls down to his shoulders. His beard is just as thick and curly, reaching his chest. This man could be Thor in a faded red checkered flannel shirt and jeans. Both were wrinkled from real work. The blisters on his hands back this up. He looks out the window of the small shack he and his bother called home. It was a shack that looked like it had been nailed together, whatever the builder could find despite this. It was sturdy. It is one room with two messy cots pushed against opposite walls. An old wood table and chairs that have seen better days sit in the middle of the room. A wood-burning stove sits beside a counter with a sink and hand pump. Camping gear has been piled up in another corner. "Royal will be watching that hill like a hawk."

"Heath, not the side we will be going up," Earl said pleadingly. "We leave early enough and will be up before the sheriff realizes it. Just follow the trail, and we are there."

"If you got it all figured out," Heath said, turning back to his brother. "You don't need me."

"Come on, you are the mountain guy. You know that mountain like the back of your hand. Think of the money."

"We both know I have never been up to her place. You were right there with me. You felt it. You felt her. She was saying get the hell away from here."

"We just have to get them there."

"Then just leave them? I doubt Miss Lang will pay us in advance," the man said with a grunt. He looked around the small room. "Oh hell, I can't live like this anymore."

"It's more money we could earn in a year....hell, ten years. We could get out of this godforsaken town. You only stayed here because of Paw and Molly. Now Paw is dead, and Molly has moved to Cornwall. With the money, we could move to Cornwall. Maybe get a job at the university. They pay real good."

"You said that one of the people is a professor from the university? Getting him up there and back might be useful. He could put a good word in for us."

"Now you're talking."

"I am not saying I am going. I want to talk to this Lang woman. Need to get some things straight."

Heath turned back to the window, thinking and ignoring the bad feeling in his gut. But his brother was right. This could be a chance to get out of Echo Hill. As far as he was concerned, the whole place was cursed, not just the mountain.

PART 2
CHAPTER 1

Heath was now dressed in a red shirt and jeans that looked new. His hair and beard were both cut really short and nicely trimmed. With all the hair gone, he was a very handsome man. He stood alone by a small creek. Across the creek was a thick wall of bushes and trees. His brother came up, hauling two packs and dropping them by his brother. He waited for a moment. "You sure this is way? It doesn't look right."

"This is it. The bushes block the path. It's why they missed it." Heath said as he nervously cracked his knuckles. He turned and watched his clients climb up the path. Audrey Lang was leading the pack, wearing jeans that were so tight that he was amazed she could walk. Her jacket, along with her pack, looked used but probably came from some high-end shop. A small woman with black hair dressed in a bright red coat and jeans that all looked new. A tall young man with long hair came up next. He was wearing a heavy pack and carrying a camera in one hand. A short woman came next, wearing a pack and carrying what he guessed was a microphone attached to a pole. Next came a chubby man who didn't look happy. As a matter of fact, he looked terrified. Then came a man who looked like he might have done some camping. He looked excited. Then came the professor, who wore all new gear like the short lady. He looked nervous, which surprised Heath.

"You must, Heath," Audrey said, walking right up to the big man. She was relieved. This man looked like he belonged out here. "I am Audrey Lang."

Heath shook her outstretched hand and smiled. Who wears perfume in the woods? Bears might wonder what that was and come looking. But bears weren't his worry. Well, one bear, maybe. He needed to get some things straight. "Miss Lang, we must get a thing or two straight."

"Heath, we all made a deal with your brother," Audrey said, giving him her famous smile.

"It is only a verbal contract, but any court will side with us," Carol said, standing beside Audrey. She let her backpack slide off her shoulders and onto the ground. So, let's be on our way."

"That supposed verbal contract wasn't made with me...."

"Hang on, Carol. Let's hear the man out," Audrey said, thinking the man just wanted more money, and he might be worth it by his look.

"All right, we all know we are trespassing onto private property. Breaking the law. When we return, my brother and I must stay here. You all can run back to Hollywood or wherever you came from. We might end up in jail. The owners are not as rich as you, but rich enough."

"Fine. You win. Triple the amount."

"I'll take it. Now listen. While we are on the trail. I call the shots. I will take you to the logging camp and Echo's house. After that, my brother and I will camp back at the logging camp while you do whatever you are going to do. Since I have seen your show, I am sure you and your people will want to stay the night."

"Yes, we will," Audrey said without hesitation.

"Wait, wait," Wolsky said, stepping forward. "You never said anything about staying the night up there. Considering the reputation of Echo Hill is that wise."

Audrey turned and looked at the professor. She might be a blonde, but she wasn't dumb, not by a long shot. She was also an excellent judge of character. This man was scared. She looked at his assistant. He looked excited and ready to go. "Alex, what do you think?"

"Professor Wolsky is just being cautious," Alex said, giving Wolsky a cool stare. He has a high respect for Echo Hill's reputation. We were led to believe this would be a quick trip. Luckily, I brought along our sleeping bags. They are in the car."

"You better go get them," Heath said, pulling out a small handheld radio. "You hold onto this and call us when you are ready to leave."

"You get us there. Camp at the lumber camp while we do our show. We call when we are ready to leave. Simple enough." Audrey said as she studied the bushes across the creek. Alex and Wolsky walk back to the cars parked down the hill. Three men were standing around the three SUVs. Audrey pointed to them. "Those men will drive our cars to the motel in another town and wait for our call. When do we leave?"

"Right now, but one thing," Heath said. "Is the man hiding in the bushes with you?"

"What?" Carol gasped and whirled around.

CHAPTER 2

THE INTRUDER

Donald Novak was one of the top psychics in the nation—at least, that's what he said on his web and YouTube channel. The twenty-three-year-old had just hit one million followers but still wasn't making the big bucks. He discovered that, like Hollywood, the real money came from endorsements. Donald was not a sexy blonde who pushed Apple products or a cute woman who taught kids how to bake desserts. He was short and a little out of shape.

His show was doing psychic readings for people on the street. He had learned all the tricks from his father. Who had learned them from his father? Yes. Tricks. Reading people's faces. Asking leading questions and looking for clues. Like wedding ring or cross hanging around their necks. You kept your insights vague or so broad they could apply to anyone. Dad had done all these on the phone and then on TV.

That was old-school

The Internet was where the money was now.

It was working for him, but he needed something. Something big. Something like Echo Hill.

Once he heard that Audrey Lang wanted to go to Echo Hill, he knew that with her money and power, it was going to happen. He just followed her producer. Thankfully, his girlfriend and ex-girlfriend had all the gear he needed. She actually charged him two hundred bucks.

Bitch.

He actually owed her the two hundred. He would be a dead man if she didn't bring back the gear.

That's how Donald squatted behind a bush, watching the group get ready to climb the mountain. His plan was simple. He would follow them up and make his videos. His stuff would be up long before Audrey's show aired.

The money would follow.

"HEY!" Donald yelled as the blonde mountain man approached and yanked him out of the bushes. He pushed him to the ground.

"Who the hell are you?" Heath barked.

"Hey, I know that guy," Jerry said, looking down at the small, chubby man. He has a show on YouTube. He's supposed to be a psychic."

"I am a psychic!" Donald snapped, climbing to his feet and brushing off the dirt and leaves on his clothes."

"What the hell are you doing here?" Carol growled, moving right into Donald's face. "You trying to screw up our show. What's the plan? Follow us and post before we can air? You little weasel!"

"All right, we have established that this guy is not part of your group," Heath said. "Let's get going. I got feeling the sheriff is close by."

"Get lost," Carol yelled and shoved Donald.

"Carol, we can't leave him here," Audrey said calmly. She moved in front of the small man and smiled. "We leave him here. He will follow or go to the sheriff. We have no choice but to take him with us. Now listen to me carefully, Donny. I have seen your show. You are nothing more than a con artist. This is my party. So my rules. You will film when and what I allow you to. You will post only when I say. If you don't. I will use all my wealth and power to crush you like a bug. Do you understand?"

"Yes," Donald said, sounding more like a child than a grown man. It was at this moment he realized the big flaw in his plan. Audrey was already wealthy. He wasn't.

"If we are done," Heath said, walking away. He pulled on a heavy pack like it weighed nothing and grabbed a rifle leaning against a tree. He checked the rifle. Alex walked up and watched him.

"What kind of rifle is that?" Donald asked.

"Winchester model 70. Alaska series." Heath said, working bolt action.

"I don't think that will be useful against what we hope to find."

"You are right about that. But this will stop a bear." Heath said with a big grin.

"There bears up there?" Wolsky asked, looking concerned.

"This Oregon, we got bears, wolves, cougars. A little bit of everything apparently ghosts. I made a deal with you. I'll protect you from the wild animals. You protect me from the ghosts." Heath said with a wink and smile. Then splashed across the creek and up to a thick green bush. One of his thick arms pushed back the branches. Like magic, a narrow path was revealed.

"Not every wide," Jerry said, thinking the trail already looked creepy.

"This is an animal path," Heath said. It's narrow and winding, but it will get you there. Relax; we're safe on the trail. It's where you're going you've got to worry about. Let's go!"

CHAPTER 3

NO GOING BACK NOW

Audrey was the first to duck under the branches and step onto the path. She took a few steps and quickly felt claustrophobic. The trees seemed to close in around her. They were thick with a rough black bark, unlike anything she had seen. The thick trunks seemed twisted and scarred, reaching up to the sky like some perverted thing not created by nature. Their branches spread into a dark green canopy, blocking most of the sun, creating a shadowy world where only a few beams of sunlight broke through. There were brushes covered with odd-shaped leaves and thorns. But the most noticeable thing was the quiet. There weren't any cheerful chirps of birds or leaves rustling by the wind. There was no wind. Just a warm air that seemed to envelop her. She stood momentarily, feeling like the forest was trying to suffocate her. For a fleeting moment, she thought about leaving. This place felt wrong...no evil. "This is a mistake....No."

A few deep breaths cleared her mind and lifted her spirit. A smile came to her lips. Audrey slowly turned, taking the dark forest. "Excellent, you are going to be my best show."

Carol came in next and stopped in her tracks. She tried to turn back but was pushed forward by Audrey. She started up the trail but didn't look happy.

Jerry stumbled in. His path was blocked by his boss.

"What?" He asked in an already breathless tone. His eyes were huge circles. Sweat was running down his face. An ashen face.

"Carol told me she had to drag your fat ass up here. You were actually going to bail on me. Bail on me. That would not be wise."

"Did she tell you what happened in my office?"

"Yes, that confirms everything, I believe," Audrey said. "You listen. This show will put me on the map. No more jokes about me being blonde and posing for the camera while pretending to hunt ghosts. You do your job, or you will find yourself back in jail."

Jerry muttered something before rushing up the trail. Wolsky and Alex came next. Alex stopped and smiled. "You give a hell of a pep talk."

"I think the professor might need one," Audrey said, watching Wolsky plod up the path.

"He'll be fine," Alex said.

"You and I are the only professionals on this trip. Can I count on you to back me up?"

"Absolutely. We are here for the same thing." He said. "The ghosts. This is our chance to prove them all wrong."

He nodded and moved on.

Todd came in carrying his camera, looking miserable.

"Todd! Why aren't you filming?" Audrey growled.

"We're not there yet..."

"This is the start of an epic adventure. You will film everything. You understand. I want everything. The hike and whatever we find. You need to use a tree. You hand the camera to someone else. I will not miss a second of this trip."

"Yes, Miss Lang," Todd said, bringing up his camera and turning it on. "I'll get everything."

"You want me to do the sound?" Maria asked.

"The camera has a mic. That will do for the trail," Audrey said. But once we are there, I count on you to pick up sounds that the average ear can't. We must not miss anything."

Heath walked up and smiled. "There's a small clearing up always. If you want to do some kind introduction."

"Thank you." She said as the big man passed. A smile came to her lips. It vanished when Donald walked up. "Just remember my party."

The psychic watched the beautiful woman continue up the trail. For the first time in his life, Donald had a genuine psychic experience.

Cool chills ran through his body, making her shiver and almost pee his pants. A very soft voice in the air said something. It sounded like go away. Donald looked back and found a nerve he didn't know he had. He slowly walked up the trail.

The hike was uneventful except for the ever-present feeling of the forest closing around them. More than once, a branch seemed to reach out and lash at them. Todd ended up with a small scratch on his cheek. There was no playful banter or jokes. Everyone just plodded along with their heads down. The depressive mood was lifted when they came into a small clearing. It was sunlit, with a small creek running through it. It was like the trees above had allowed the sun to peek through this small area. There was even a fallen log to sit on.

Everyone pulled off their packs and slumped to the ground. Even Heath looked a little weary. He went to the creek and splashed watch onto his face. Audrey joined him and asked. "How far to the house?"

"The logging camp is a little over an hour, and the house another half hour," Heath said with a smile. You can feel it, too. Can't you?"

"Yes, I can feel her," Audrey said, looking up at the trees in awe. "What kind of trees are these?"

"They are supposed to be black oak. But I have never seen oaks like these. You're not thinking Echo is happy to have you here?"

"No, she is not. That's why we must be cautious," she said. Then she stood up and walked over to Todd and Marie, who were sipping water. "All right, I want to do a quick intro. Then we move on."

An icy wind blew through the clearing, throwing some leaves into the air. The almost black leaves seemed to drift into the air, hang there, and float to the ground. Audrey smiled at Todd. "That's why you keep filming."

Audrey and Walt were the only happy ones in the group.

CHAPTER 4

MADE THEIR BED

Sheriff Adam Royal watched his deputy, Josh, push back the branches. He was holding a phone to his ear. A deep sigh came from his lips. "Mr. Wilkins, we found it. It was just where you thought it might be. There is an old beat-up Honda down the road. No other cars."

Josh knelt down and studied the ground. He was a hunter, so he knew how to track. He looked up and said, "Fresh tracks. At least a half dozen people. Pretty fresh."

"Yeah, they are already headed up. Do you want us to follow?"

"No." the man on the other end of the signal snapped so loud Josh could hear it. Then, more quietly. "I don't want you or your deputy to risk your lives. I've checked with my lawyers. They are there illegally. You warned them. What happens is their own fault. Call the Burton brothers. Hire them to watch the trail in case someone comes down. Double their usual rate. Make sure they understand to not go up the trail."

"Trust me, those boys will watch the trail and all they do. Like most people around her. They have a healthy respect for Echo Hill."

"Call me when it is set up. Adam, you did a good job."

Jake walked up. "Please tell me we don't have to go up there."

"Not today. Maybe in a day or two."

"To get the bodies?"

"Yup, get the bodies."

CHAPTER 4

A MURDER OF CROWS

"We are now on Echo Hill," Audrey said into the camera. Her long hair was now loose around her face. She looked around the clearing and then back at the camera. "We are at a clearing about one hour from the logging camp. This was the camp built by Harry Johnson. According to reports, the sawmill is unfinished, but the bunkhouse is. There have been no reports of any paranormal activity at the camp, but that doesn't mean they haven't been. Remember. We are the first real professional paranormal researchers to come to Echo Hill. Unlike others in the past. We will make no mistakes."

"And cut!" Carol said with a nod. "Perfect. Well, I guess we should move on."

"I thought that writer guy was a professional ghost hunter," Todd asked.

"He was," Alex said, coming up. "Well respected. He retired after Echo Hill. Now makes quite a lot of money writing horror novels."

"If he was a pro..." Todd said.

"Walt Wilkins did it as a hobby," Audrey said, walking up. "We do this full-time and have better equipment. Heath, if you would lead the way."

Wolsky stood looking up the trail. To him, it looked like a dark tunnel leading to...to what? Donald came up beside him. "This place is not what I expected."

"What did you expect?" Wolsky asked.

"I didn't expect to find any real ghosts. But there are, and they are watching us."

"Are you really a psychic?"

"Apparently, I am now." The psychic said with a small smile. He was trying to ignore the voices in his head and the growing fear in his belly. "Daddy would be so proud."

"Gentlemen, ladies, the trail awaits," Heath said, moving past them and up the trail. Audrey and Carol followed. Todd stopped, filming Maria and Earl, who walked by. Alex came up and slammed Wolsky's pack into his stomach. Then, he went up the trail.

"You guys go on," Todd said. "I am supposed to bring up the rear."

The two men pulled on their backs and walked into the dark forest. Todd lowered his camera and was tempted to run back down the trail. He could see the spinning reels in his mind. His eyes closed.

"TODD!"

They popped open at the sound of Audrey's voice. He started to film and walk at the same time.

The next hour seemed so much longer. The trees became more oppressive, if that was possible. There were times when the daylight seemed to vanish. They blindly walked in darkness ever forward despite the growing uneasiness in themselves. Time again, the branches seemed to reach out and scratch them. The glowing eyes of unseen animals peeked out at them from the shadows. A fear settled on most of the party. Only Audrey and Alex seemed to be immune to the effects of the trees surrounding them.

They continued onward and upward on the winding trail until they came into a vast open area. They all stopped at the path's end.

The logging camp was a large clearing with two wooden structures from another era. A long log house with broken windows and an open door. The other building was made of logs but unfinished. There were three walls. This one had a wooden water wheel that slowly rotated with low creaking. There was a long, flat table down the middle. Despite their age, the buildings were in good shape. There was no evidence of the forest taking back this area. The small compound seemed to be shrouded in shadows.

But it wasn't the camp that was holding the group's attention.

It was the crows. The tops of buildings, the unfinished framework of the sawmill, the branches of the trees even on the ground. There were crows. Hundreds of crows. Just perked and stared at the newcomers. They didn't move or make a sound of any kind. Their black eyes just looked without blinking.

"What the hell," Wolsky muttered.

"Todd." Audrey snapped.

"I'm getting it," Todd said, now regretting not escaping when he had the chance. This was right out of that old Hitchcock movie.

Maria and Carol pulled out cameras and started to take pictures. Alex pulled out his own video camera and started to film. Heath and Earl glanced at each other.

"We should have asked for more money," Earl said.

"A little late now, little brother," Heath muttered, thinking there was no place he rather than back in that crummy old shack. His grip tightens on the rifle in his hands. "We are in the lion's den now."

CHAPTER 5

LAST WARNING

The only sounds came from clicking cameras and soft wind through the trees. Audrey and Alex are the only ones who look excited. Both have big smiles and chat among themselves, oblivious to the fear the rest of the party is experiencing.

"What do we do now?" Jerry asked, glancing back at the trail.

"We film!" Audrey said with an even bigger smile. "Todd on me."

Todd quickly aims the camera at his boss and nods. Audrey motions to the crows. "Ladies and gentlemen, we have arrived at the logging camp. As you see. We have crows. Lots of crows. Not moving or even making a sound. As many of you know, crows are seen as an omen of bad luck. Could the Echo Hill witch be warning us off? Could it be she is giving us the chance to leave? Could the Echo Hill witch be not totally evil? Of course, we will not be leaving. Not until we reach the home of Echo Hacker."

Suddenly, the crows explode life. The caws sound like the roar of angry animals. Their flapping wings and caw fill the air as the birds launch into the air. They begin to swirl around and around, looking more like a black cloud than a murder of crows. Then, they began to swoon down. Not in two or three but dozens. Even Audrey screams as the party drops to the ground, trying to avoid the low-flying crows. Carol and Maria are sobbing. As some of the crows pick at their clothes and packs. Audrey stops screaming and peeks over her arms. Her green eyes filled with fear and fascination. Alex's face is buried in the dirt, and his arms are over his head. Todd has his face down, but his camera is still pointed up. The snowstorm seems to go on for hours.

Then, like magic, the crows are gone.

"Wow. That was intense." Alex said, climbing to his feet.

Audrey goes over to Todd and grabs the camera. She fiddles with it while looking at the view screen. A smile comes to her lips. "Excellent. You got it. You got yourself a bonus."

Todd takes back the camera and helps Maria get to her feet. "I just hope I get to spend it."

Carol gets up and dusts herself off. Then she runs after her boss. Audrey, we've got enough. We've got the logging camp and crows..."

"You are not going to suggest we go back down the hill," Audrey asks, looking at Carol. This is the tip of the iceberg. We do some quick shots here, get something to eat, and then onward."

"There is a creek by the sawmill," Heath said after walking over. If you want to clean up, the house is only a half hour away, but I suggest we rest and eat."

"I was thinking the same thing," Audrey said, patting his arm and grinning. "Get us to the house, and you'll get a bonus."

"Thank you," he said, and like Todd, he hoped he would get to spend it. Heath walks over to his brother and dusts off his back. We will leave our packs here. It will make the hike easier. We will be all right camping here.

"I think I am going to stay with them," Earl said, not looking at his brother, who was licking his lips.

"What the hell?" Heath said in a soft voice. Did you just miss the crows? I don't believe in ghosts and such, but this place is wrong. We agreed to stay here."

"This is huge. We are making history here." Earl said, watching Audrey brush out her hair while Todd set up the shot. "It's our way out of here."

Heath notices who his brother is watching and lets off a deep sigh. "Brother, you are thinking you have a chance with that woman. The daughter of a billionaire with a body and looks like that. You ain't dreaming; you are crazy. We are just hired help."

"I know that, but we'll get her back down the mountain with her pictures and stuff. She's going to be grateful."

"Not that grateful. Do what you please." Heath snaps and walks off.

Jerry and Carol sit on the steps of the unfinished house. They watch the water wheel slowly turn. Both are sipping watches and sandwiches. Jerry nudges her, " This is what you expected?"

"No," Carol growls while shaking her head. "This is not like the places we have gone. This feels different. It feels real."

"Tell me about it. Look at Audry. She acted like the crows were no big deal. We should leave now. We got enough for the show."

"You heard her. She wants to see the house. Let's hope she will be satisfied with seeking it and taking some pictures."

Preston sat alone, sipping water and staring into the woods. Yes, he was afraid, but he kept hearing a soft and sweet woman's voice. He couldn't understand the words, but despite their sweetness, he knew they were threats.

Alex walked around the camp holding a small red device in his hand. He would stop to look at the EMF meter. Wolsky watched him while munching on his sandwich. Finally, he got up and walked over. "Are you picking anything up?"

"I was at first, but it's dropped to normal," Alex said, moving close to the water wheelhouse. The device beeped. "A little higher here. That is interesting."

"Alex, you actually think they're ghosts here?"

"Not here, but close by. This is amazing. We could be on the verge of proving life after death. That ghosts are real. This is historic."

"Alex, if it turns out, there is a ghost up here. That means the stories are true. Which means she will kill us."

"No. No. Echo knows we are here to study her. We not to harm her or her precious hill or house. We are here to learn."

"I think your enthusiasm is clouding your judgment. I may not believe in this, but I know the history of this place. Echo Hacker kills people."

"Okay, on me," Audrey said, striking a pose in front of the log house. Todd nods while Maria holds the mike over her boss' head. "As you have seen. We have the first evidence that Echo Hill's legends may be real. The crows may have been a warning for us to stay away. But I don't believe that. I think Echo Hacker was showing her power. Telling us to respect her. She has to know we are here to learn. We want her to teach us."

Todd and Maria glance at each other and roll their eyes.

"Is it too late to quit?" Maria asked.

"You really think she will let us leave. Besides, we go back down the mountain, and she goes missing." Todd said, looking serious. "Who do you think her billionaire father is going to blame?"

"Talk about being screwed."

CHAPTER 6

COLD SPOT

The hike to the house was uneventful and thankfully short. The path actually seemed brighter with the sun high overhead. Heath stopped at the edge of what appeared to be a perfectly round clearing. Tall, dark trees are pressing against the clearing like some invisible force is holding them back.

In the middle of the clearing is an A-framed house made of logs with a thatched roof. There are four windows on each side of the cabin. Three steps go up to the porch at the front of the house. There is a thick wood door with some kind of carving mounted into it. Facing the house is a small barn. A simple structure with a V-roof and double doors. A broken-down fence surrounding something is on the other side of the clearing. The place looks old but in surprisingly good shape.

"This is it," Heath said, waving his hand toward the house but staying off the clearing. "Call me when you need me."

"You're just leaving us?" Audrey asked when the big man turned to leave. She is more amused than annoyed. "I would think you would at least be curious."

"Miss Lang, I learned a long time ago. You don't poke a bear. This was the deal. I got you here. I will get you down when you are ready." Heath said, looking back at the house. "I know you can feel it. This place is evil."

"Thank you for your honesty," Audrey said with a smile. She actually liked this man. He didn't seem intimated by her wealth or beauty. It was something to think about once they got off this hill. "I respect that. I'll call when we are ready."

"My brother is staying. Take care, Miss Lang."

"Call me Audrey."

"I will just be a radio call away...Audrey," he said with a smile and walked down the trail. The big man walked away but glanced back. She was a fine-looking woman.

Audrey watched him go but then turned back to the clearing. She rubbed her hands together, stepped into the clearing, and gasped. Her arms quickly wrapped around her body. "My God, it's freezing?"

Alex pulls off his pack and removes his EMF detector and another device. He steps out into the clear and gasps. Shivering, he looks at the devices. EMF is beeping. Its green light flashes. Clouds come out of his mouth as he speaks. "This place is hot. I have never seen readings this high. This is the real deal. This entire place is a cold spot."

Audrey rushes over and looks at his devices. They both laugh. Then Audrey glares at Todd. "You better be filming this!"

"Yeah, yeah," Todd said, holding up the camera. "I am getting everything.

Audrey and Alex begin to move across the clearing toward the house. Carol lets off a deep groan and follows but stops when the cold hit her. "MY GOD! IT'S FREEZING."

Todd and Marie step in, gasping but rushing to catch up with their boss. Now, only Jerry, Earl, and Preston wait. Finally, they step into the clearing. They gasp and wrap their arms around their bodies. Earl pulls off his pack, digs through it, and finds a jacket.

Audrey and Alex reach the house, stopping to take it in. They both pull off their packs as they take in the giant head of a wolf carved into the door. The detail is impressive, right down to what looks like real teeth in its open mouth, but the red eyes really creep you out. Todd and Maria come up behind them.

"That is pretty creepy," Todd said. "Why would anyone crave that into a door?"

"Protection," Audrey said.

"It didn't do any good."

"Against evil spirits." Audrey glared back at her cameraman. "She was murdered by men. And they all paid for their crime with their lives."

"Another reason to be leaving," Todd mutters.

The rest of the group comes up and stares at the house. Carol steps up by Audrey. "So we going in?"

"No," Audrey said, looking back at the barn. "We will set up in the barn. I want to be ready for anything. "Alex, is it getting warm?"

"Yes," Alex said, looking at his devices. The EMFs have dropped but are still strong."

"Perhaps she was giving us another warning," Preston said, looking quite pale. "I suggest we be very, very..."

"Careful," Todd said.

"No. Respectful. This is Echo's home."

CHAPTER 7

FIRST MISTAKE

Jerry had set up his computers on an old table that wasn't too wobbly. He was sitting on an old wooden box, using his jacket to make it more comfortable. The setup was right before the barn doors, giving him a good view of the house.

The barn had two stalls and a loft. Its dirt floor was weed-free and surprisingly clean. It was decided that they would sleep in the barn while the others rolled out their sleeping bags and used two old boxes as tables for their food. Earl had built a small campfire just outside the barn. It was being used to make coffee.

Audrey stayed by the doors, watching the house. Alex was checking his equipment. Todd and Carol discussed how many mini cams to set up around the location. Maria busied herself with the sound gear but kept glancing at the house. A fallen Catholic, she was tempted to make the sign of the cross but wasn't sure if that would do more harm than good. Preston stood by the fire, staring at the broken-down fence across the clearing.

"That's a graveyard," Preston said more to himself than Earl.

"What?" Earl said, looking up from the fire.

"Over there. It's the family graveyard. I will take a look."

"You may want to check with Miss Lang first," Earl said, standing up with the coffee pot. "It is her party."

"Yes, it is." He said, not taking his eyes off the graveyard.

Earl walked away, stopping by Audrey. "Coffee is ready."

"Wonderful." Audrey glanced at him but then returned her gaze to the house. "Can you feel it?"

"I can feel something, Miss Lang," Earl said. "Ain't sure what it is. Thinking my brother had the right idea."

"No, he was right to leave. He was giving off a negative energy. Still, I like him. What did Preston say to you?"

"He wants to take a look at the graveyard."

"Good, it will keep him out of the way. The house is the real hot spot. Think about it. We may be the first to step inside for God knows how long."

"I thought that writer went inside."

"He has no evidence to prove he did. I suspect he only went as far as the logging camp. You know he and his wife barely got back alive." Then she frowns. "But they did see and find something."

"How do you know that?" Earl said, looking back at the house.

"Neither he nor his wife has ever come back. Something scared them," Audrey said with a smile. And I want to know what it was."

"Maybe we won't be so lucky."

"They were amateurs. I'm a professional. I ain't afraid of no ghost."

Earl didn't care for her casual attitude. She took the coffee pot and walked back into the barn. Earl was so focused on the house that he didn't watch her walk away.

A short time later, Audrey and Alex examined the wolf's head while Todd filmed. Maria stood by the side with her Mike. Wolsky and Earl stood at the bottom of the stairs. Carol had opted to stay in the barn with Jerry.

"The detail is amazing," Alex said, taking a few pictures and then using the EMF to scan it. "Nothing."

"But there was," Audrey said, running her hands over her head and fingering the fangs. She glanced up at the house. "These are really sharp. My God, the eyes are some kind of jewels. I don't think they are glass."

"If they are rubies. They are big rubies."

This got Earl's attention. He nudged Wolsky and asked. "Did they say rubies?"

"Yes, yes." He said, looking nervous but interested. "It could set me up for life."

"The rubies?"

"No, no. This place. I just have to get back."

"Let's see what's inside," Audrey said, pushing on one door while Alex pushed open the other door. The door creaked but quickly swung open. They stepped into a large room with a ladder that ran up to a loft. An old brass bed sat up in the loft. Thick wood beams ran across the ceiling. A massive stone fireplace dominates the back of the room. A cast iron grate sat in the firebox. Two orate claws were mounted in front to hold the logs in place. One rocking chair sat on a thin rug in front of the fireplace. The only other furniture was a table with one chair. Some pots, pans, dishes, and cups rested on the one shelf mounted on the wall. Hanging from the ceiling is a chandelier made of deer antlers. Aside from the dusty floor and some spider webs up in the rafters. The room was surprisingly clean. "This doesn't look too bad."

Audrey and Alex step into the room and wander around. Alex uses his EMF while Audrey moves to the shelf. She studies the items. Finally, picking up a cup and turning it over. "My God, this was hers."

Alex's device emits a low beep. He looks over and smiles. "I don't think she likes you touching her stuff."

"I'm the same way." She said carefully, putting the cup back and moving to the front of the room. Audrey runs her fingers over the mantle, looks at the dust on her fingers, and wipes it off on her jeans. She steps toward the chair, but a creaking sound from the floor makes her stop. She rocks back and forth on her heels. The squealing continues. Audrey moves the chair and pulls back the rug. There is a trapdoor built into the floor. She looks at Alex. "I found a trapdoor."

"What?" Alex runs over and kneels down beside Audrey. They both smile at each other. "It could just be a root cellar."

"Probably just a root cell," Audrey said. "Let's open it."

Audrey looks around and spots the rest of the team still standing outside the door. Her face flushes with anger. "TODD! I told you to follow me. Film everything! Get over here now!"

Todd and Maria glance at each other. A loud crack of thunder makes them both jump. The blue sky is gone. Black clouds rolled above, putting the entire clearing into dark shadows. The once beautiful trees now look much more threatening. A black wall surrounds them. They glance up at them. Then each other. A light rain begins. This makes them walk into the house. Earl and Wolsky follow. They all look around as they move toward the trapdoor. A clicking sound makes them stop and look up.

"Rats?" Maria asked.

"Are there rats in the woods?" Todd asked.

"Like I would know," Maria said.

"It's the rain," Wolsky said, sounding like he was trying to convince himself than the others.

Another yell makes them rush over to the trapdoor.

"We heard something. Maybe rats." Todd said.

"We are in the woods. Animals live in the woods. On me and Alex." Audrey said. They both pull on the iron ring. It takes a few pulls to get it open. It slams back on the floor. Everyone peers down into the black hole. A steep, narrow staircase runs down into the hole. "I don't think this is a root cellar."

"We need to get our flashlights," Alex said.

"Absolutely," Audrey said. "Earl, be a nice guy and get our flashlights. Oh, better the headlamps. Hurry."

Earl runs off. Todd peers down into the hole and asks. "So we are going down into the big scary hole in the ground."

"Of course," Audrey said, looking up in disbelief.

We should set up cameras before we do that. Todd asked. "It won't take long."

"You're right. Set up two cameras down here. One up in the loft. Get the cameras with night vision. We will need those for the tunnel. Maria, you will stay up here. The mike pole will be in the way. We do a sound check once we are down there."

"If I put a receiver on the bottom step, we should be fine." Maria looks very happy. Todd glares at her. She sticks out her tongue.

CHAPTER 8

THE BLIND PSYCHIC

Preston is still standing by the doors, looking at the graveyard. The rain was now coming down even harder. He frowns when Earl comes running out and into the barn. He starts to grab the flashlights and headlamps. Carol watches while Jerry stays focused on the computer screen. He looks excited now. "They found a tunnel. They are going down."

"They will need to set up cameras first," Carol snaps. And they will need cameras with night vision. We need this all on video."

Looking annoyed, she goes to one of the packs and pulls out several small cameras. Earl runs back toward the house. "Hey, you need to take these."

Earl just runs through the rain and back into the house.

"Looks like you get to go in," Jerry said with a shrug.

"I will be right back," Carol growls and heads out of the barn. She stops and looks up. It seems even darker. The rain is like standing in a shower. The ground is quickly turning to mud. "Great rain. Just what we need."

"It's Oregon," Preston said, pulling on a rain poncho. "It rains here."

"I hate rain. It is one of the reasons I live in Los Angeles," Carol said, pulling on a jacket that would be useless in the rain. She grabbed the gear and ran toward the house.

Preston watches her go into the house. He glances back at Jerry. "I am going to the graveyard. Audrey said I could check it out."

"In this rain," Jerry said, typing away on his keyboard. He glances up, but Preston is gone.

Preston slowly walks across the compound, obviously surrounded by the rain. He reaches the broken-down fence. There were thirteen small graves, perfectly shaped mounds outlined by white stones. Identical same tombstones with no dates or names. Words like Mother,

Father, Sister, Brother, Uncle, and Aunt are etched into some stones. The rest are blank.

The rain pounds down on the graves. The water bounces off them like dirt mounds are made of rock, keeping their perfect shape. Small pools form around the graves. After a while, streams begin to flow away from the graves.

Preston stands like a statue, watching the graves. Dirt on one of the graves with a blank stone begins to slowly wash away. The face appears in the mud. More skull than face. The psychic steps forward and watches the white face appear. Very slowly, he walks into the graveyard. He stops at the foot of the grave. He wipes away the rain on his face as he drops to his knees. Then he is on his hands and knees, crawling over the grave to look right down into the skull-like face. His breathing becomes hard and fast. He wants to get up but can't. "No. No. No."

Entire eyeballs appear in the sockets of the skull face. They are yellow with big black pupils. The bare teeth seemed to spread into a smile. Then, a screeching voice fills his head. "Do you believe now?"

"NOOOOO!" Preston pulls back up. Skeleton's hands come out to grab his head. The skull face comes up and looks into his. Their faces are almost touching. He screams while the skull laughs. A snake-like tongue comes out and rolls across his face. Then, he is pulled down into the muddy grave. Preston struggles as his face is pulled into the mud. The helpless man is now lying on the grave. His arms and legs thrashing around. Slowly, he is pulled into the grave. His head and shoulders sink into the mud. Slowly, the rest of his body is pulled into the grave. Preston chokes as the mud fills his mouth. It runs into his ear, cutting all sound but his muffled screams. Then, suddenly, he is no longer in the mud. He is lying in darkness. Preston can barely move. He is in some kind of box. He screams as he hits the top of the box. The sound of the rain sounds more like soft thudding. Then he realizes the sound is coming from above him. The reality hits him. He is in a coffin buried six feet from the surface. His screams become louder and more frantic, but no one can hear him.

Jerry looks up at a muffled sound, listens, and returns to the computer screen.

CHAPTER 9

SECOND MISTAKE

Todd is placing a small camera just over the door. He wipes the lens. Satisfied, he holds up his hand radio. "How's the picture?"

"Perfect," Jerry said. "With this one and another, we cover the entire room. One more in the loft, and we will be ready. Have fun in the dark evil looking hole."

"Yeah, thanks," Todd said. He jumped down and walked over to the ladder leading to the loft. He glanced over at the group standing by the hole. Only Audrey and Alec seemed excited. "We should not go into that hole. We should leave."

He climbs up the ladder, which creaks. Todd stops and debates if this is a good idea.

"Todd, move it. We are losing light." Audrey yells, adjusting her headlamp. She looks down into the hole. "The walls are just dirt, but the floor is paved with stones. I think this is more than a root cellar."

Todd once again debates but finally climbs up the ladder. He reaches the loft and looks around for a spot. Finally, he puts one over the brass bed and sniffs. "Is that lavender?"

The bed is in perfect shape, as is the black and red quilt covering it. Todd kneels on the bed and starts to mount the camera. He looks down at the bed and frowns. He hits the bed with a fist. No dust flies up. Now, I am more than a little scared. He finishes and climbs off the bed.

"Todd."

Todd whirls around at the sound of his name. He stares at the bed. The quilt is now pressed down like someone is lying on it. He staggers back. The ghostly form of a woman appears. Her hair and body have a green tint to it. The incredibly long hair floats around her naked body. As her face becomes more explicit, so does her beauty. She reaches out with one hand, smiling, and whispers. "Come to me. I want you."

"NOOOO!" Todd falls back onto the floor and crawls to the ladder without looking back. He manages to climb but falls to the floor and scurries away for the loft. "NO! NO! GET AWAY FROM ME!"

Audrey and Alex run over. They kneel down and stop him. It appears they are going to comfort him. Then they both look up. Audrey asked. "What happened?"

"The reading on my EMF shot up," Alec said, holding up the device. "What did you see?"

"I SAW HER! I SAW HER!" Todd screams and sobs, still trying to get to the door. "SHE WAS IN THE BED. SHE WANTED ME. I AM GETTING OUT OF HERE!"

"You saw an actual ghostly apparition?" Alex asked, sounding even more excited.

"Was the camera mounted and working?" Audrey asked, but when Todd didn't answer, she slapped him, which seemed to calm him down.

"What? What? The camera is working. I got to go. We have to leave now."

"Todd, we are not leaving," Audrey said. "She didn't threaten you, did she?"

Before Todd can answer. Jerry's voice comes out of her hand radio. "Audrey, you got to see this. Like now."

CHAPTER 10

THIRD MISTAKE

Everyone is crowded around Jerry's computer. All eyes are on the screen. The ghostly image of Echo fills it. Todd is in the shot, looking terrified. Then, he is out of the shot. We hear him screaming and practically falling down the ladder. The beautiful face looks right into the camera. Then, it is gone.

"Oh my god, my god," Audrey said, laughing like a child on Christmas morning. Alex is just as excited. Wolsky looks more confused than afraid. Carol, Todd, and Maria look terrified. Earl is at the back of the group. You can see the fear growing inside of him. "We actually got a ghost on camera!"

"Proof that there is life after death." Alex laughed.

"She is totally hot," Jerry said. "I will give her that. Why did she come on, Todd?"

"Miss Lang, I didn't sign up for this," Earl said, moving over to his sleeping bag. He began stuffing it into the bag. "This just got too real. I'll wait for you down with my brother."

"Fine, fine. We won't need you right now," Audrey said in a distracted tone. Tell Heath to be ready to leave. We might not have to spend the night."

"Audrey," Carol said, moving up beside Audrey. "We should leave. We have more than enough for the show. We could do the whole season based on what we have now. The crows. The images of the logging camp and the house. We got what we came for."

"What? You want to leave?" Audrey looks at the woman in shock and disbelief. "We still have the tunnel. Who knows what else we will find?"

"We...I mean, Todd just saw a ghost." Carol said.

"Did she threaten him or hurt him? No. She looked more than friendly. Todd had yet to lose his balls. He could gotten laid."

"I don't want to go into bed with a ghost." Todd snapped.

"Dude, she was totally hot," Jerry said with a laugh. "See those boobs. Way out of your league."

"Not funny. I have seen enough horror movies to know getting it on with a ghost never ends well. Boss, we should go."

"The only place we are going," Audrey growled. "Is down into that tunnel."

"Audrey, this is crazy," Carol said.

"Audrey is right," Alex said. "We are in no danger. Like Jerry said. Echo was more than friendly. You have to understand how important this is."

"I think we should stay." Wolsky quietly said, making Alex turn and look at him. "This is important. It will validate all Alex and I's research."

"My Man!" Alex comes over and hugs him. Then he pulls back. "This is going to be a hell of a book—a best seller."

"Absolutely. We have to stay."

"You people are crazy," Earl said, pulling his pack and heading for the door. "I'll be down at the lumber camp with my brother."

"That's a Good idea," Audrey said, pointing at him. Tell him to be ready to leave, or we may stay an extra day."

"An extra day!" Carol gasps.

"NO WAY!" Todd yells.

"Miss Lang…" Maria starts to say.

"Triple your hourly rate," Audrey said with a grin. "Plus, double the Christmas bonus you got last year."

"Sweet!" Jerry said, clapping his hands and then going back to the computer.

Todd, Marie, and Carol don't look happy. Earl shakes his head and goes out into the rain. Audrey thinks and then says, "Actually, only Alex and I have to enter the tunnel. We have headcams with night vision. You did bring them?"

"Yeah, yeah," Todd said, sounding calmer. "Okay, if I don't have to go in the tunnel...or the loft. I'll stay."

"We do the tunnel," Carol said, looking into Audrey's face. Stay the night. Then, in the morning, we discuss staying longer."

"Fine, let me get some coffee," Audrey said. "Todd, get the gear. Where is Preston?"

"He went to look at the graveyard," Jerry said, not looking up from his computer. That's weird, guys."

"Just as long as he is not in my way?"

"Alex, I am coming into the tunnel," Wolsky said.

"Look at you. Excellent. This will be great." Alex said.

"I have my doubts about that," Todd mutters.

CHAPTER 11

TOO LATE TO LEAVE

Earl moves down the trail with head down and shoulders hunched. His arms are wrapped around his chest as the rain unmercifully pounds down. He mutters to himself how crazy those people were. Earl comes to a divide in the trail. There are two paths leading in different directions. "What the hell? There's not supposed to be two trails."

The guide stands in the rain, shivering, debating which way to go. A crack of thunder makes him look up. He jumps up and stares into the sky. "I JUST WANT TO GO HOME!"

A deep rumbling sound comes from the trees that now seem even closer. For a few short seconds, it sounds like a woman laughing. Terrified. Earl picks a trail, moving as quickly as possible, but the mud gets softer and deeper. Soon, Earl panted as he struggled down the path. His pace is slowed as he keeps pulling his boots out of the mud. The tree branches surround him. They lash at his face and body. His panting has turned into whimpering. As he struggles up the trail, he shreds his pack and falls to his knees. Earl is now crawling on his hands and knees through the mud. He looks around at a loud, oozing sound. A low wave of mud rolls toward him. Earl screams as he frantically tries to swim through the mud. The muddy wave doesn't cover him but pushes off the trail and over a steep ridge. He claws at the muddy ground as he slides down. Earl gets a good grip on a root and slowly pulls him up. He gets to his knees when a mighty blast of wind throws him back against another tree. A sharp branch comes through his chest. Earl looks at the bloody thing sticking out his chest and screams. Blood gushes from the wound and dribbles out of his mouth. He manages to yell for his brother.

CHAPTER 12

BEAR AND MUD

Heath is standing in the doorway of the long hut, watching the rain. There is a look of concern on his face. Rivers of muddy water run through the camp. He is holding his rifle in his hands. A loud scream makes him jump. Then he stares into the night. "Little brother, was that you?"

The big man almost steps out of the hut but stops with one foot just about the muddy ground. He watches and listens. Then he steps back and jacks a shell into his rifle. "I don't know what you are, but I can smell and hear you."

A low grunting sound comes from the surrounding woods. This is followed by the sounds of rustling and more grunts. Every so slowly, something moves into the clearing. Its red eyes are the first things to appear. The large black shape lumbers closer. It is a giant black bear. It rears up and growls with its paws over its head.

"Damn, if you aren't the biggest bear I have ever seen, and I have seen a lot of them," Heath mutters as he brings up the rifle. "Why don't you be smart and move on. I got no call to shoot you yet."

The monster roars. Then drops to all fours and stares at Heath. The red eyes seem to glow. Another roar, and it charges.

Heath takes aim and fires one shot. The bear stumbles but keeps coming. He fires off three more shots in rapid succession. The bear seems to hurt but keeps coming. Heath takes careful aim and fires. One of the bear's eye explode. He quickly takes out the other eye. Another careful aim. This shot sends the bear's head down to the mud. Its colossal body follows. His hard breathing can still be heard. Heath quickly reloads, aims, and fires three shots into the bear's head. The breathing stops. He looks at the dead bear and then up at the sky. "You think I am going out there to check. It ain't happening."

Suddenly, a woman who is nothing but bones and rotting skin appears behind him. Her skin is green and yellow, with black slime running down her thin frame. Long hair drenched with more slime runs down to her knees. The thing screams as he pushes Heath out into the mud.

Heath hits the muddy ground but manages to roll onto his knees. He aims at the ghostly form, but she vanishes. A gurgling sound surrounds the hunter. He looks around, and human forms push out of the mud. It is hard to tell if they are men or women with the mud covering their faces and bodies. They begin to scream as they start to crawl toward Heath. He fires at one. It exploded like a balloon and is gone. Heath takes out a few more as he moves back from the creatures. His rifle clicks empty. He starts to pat his pockets and mutters a curse. Still moving back from the mud, he uses the rifle like a club. It is less effective than a bullet, but it works. But more and more of the things come out the muddy.

Heath ends up in the unfinished mill. The waterwheel is spinning impossibly fast. He backs up, still using the rifle as a club as he backs up. Mud begins to ooze through the floorboards. The floor is soon covered with mud as he smashes more and more of the mud creatures while trying to keep his balance. He reaches the edge of the building and looks back. The creek is now a raging river. The waterwheel is spinning even faster, wobbling like it is ready to fly off at any second. Muddy claws smash through the mud-covered floor and begin to grab at his legs. Heath stumbles, curses the things, and leaps into the river. He is quickly engulfed by the fast-moving water.

CHAPTER 13

PRETTY EVIL

Audrey is gulping down a cup of coffee between taking bites of a sandwich. Wolsky is sipping coffee while watching Todd fit a headcam around Alex's head. Carol stands over Jerry, clicking through the cameras they set up in the house. Maria is slumped against the wall, fiddling with her gear.

"Is that too tight?" Todd asks.

"No., that's good," Alex said, nodding and walking to the coffee pot.

"Okay, professor, you are next," Todd said, picking up another headcam.

"Well, everything seems nice and quiet," Jerry said as he clicked through the cameras.

"Wait, what's that?" Carol asked, pointing to the screen. "Zoom in. By the trapdoor."

"Hold on," Jerry muttered as he hit some keys. The screen now shows a white mist floating above the open trapdoor. "Dust? This place is really old. How long since that thing has been opened."

"Yeah, you're right," Carol said, sucking her lower lip. "I'm just a little nervous."

Jerry glances out the open barn doors and watches the rain. "That guy must be getting soaked out there."

"Don't worry about him," Audrey said, coming over and looking at the screen. "Worry about keeping an eye on this screen. I don't want anything missed."

"Okay, Audrey," Todd said, coming over with a headcam. He placed it on her head and adjusted the headband. Okay, you are set."

"Okay, let's do this." Audrey pulled on a poncho and looked around. "Alex, the professor, and I are in the tunnel. Todd and Maria up top. Carol, you keep an eye on everything."

"You need us in the house?" Todd asked, not sounding happy.

"Triple time with a bonus. You're in the house." Audrey snapped and walked out into the rain. Alex and Wolsky quickly followed. Maria and Todd pull on ponchos and follow.

Carol grabs a poncho and pulls it on. The picks up a hand radio. "I am going make sure they get in. You see anything. Yell!"

Jerry watches while shaking my head. "This is one time I am glad to be left behind. Why are we still here? We have enough. This is just like one of those stupid movies where one character makes everyone stay."

A loud crack of thunder makes him look up. Looking down, he sees a young woman with incredibly long blonde hair. She is wearing a very tight tee shirt and cutoffs. The pounding rain has soaked her clothes. She pushes her hair away from her face, revealing a beautiful face with bright green eyes. The young woman shyly steps into the barn. "Who are you? What are you doing here?"

"We are filming a TV show," Jerry said, unable to take his eyes off the beautiful woman. "You lost or something?"

"Yes, lost." She said, moving closer. "I live in a town close by. Some friends and I snuck up here. It started to rain, and we got separated. So this is Echo Hill. Now I am sorry we came up here."

"Me too." Jerry jumps up and steps forward. "You want some coffee? It's hot."

"That would be wonderful." She said, now shivering and moving a few steps into the barn. Jerry grabs a jacket off the back of his chair and quickly puts it around her shoulders. She shivers again. "Thank you. You are very kind. Why did you come here?"

"It's my job. We hunt ghosts." Jerry said carefully, ushering the young woman back into the barn. "Not really. We never find anything...until today."

"You found ghosts?" She asks, smiling up at Jerry.

"Maybe I found something. Oh, the coffee." He said, running over to the pot and pouring her a cup. He handed it to her with a nervous smile. You can wait here if you want. Maybe your friends will show up."

"Maybe...maybe not. You know, I heard that someone hung themselves in this barn. I guess whoever they went crazy and just hung themselves...or maybe it was Echo."

"My money is on Echo. From what I read, she was a little crazy."

The woman's face stiffens. "Maybe she was just protecting her home from trespassers."

Behind Jerry, rope begins to slither out from one of the stalls. It moves like a snake across the ground.

"Well, yeah," Jerry said. "It is terrible what happened to her. Harry Johnson did kill her and steal her land."

"Harry and his drunken friends did more than kill her. They all took their turns. She begged them to stop, but they just laughed." The woman's face grows cold and hard. "They had to pay."

The rope slithers closer while another end floats up toward an overhead beam. Jerry is so focused on the woman he doesn't notice it.

Jerry asked. "I didn't see that in any of my research. I know Harry and his friends killed her, but I didn't do an extensive study of this place."

"Maybe you just looked in the wrong place," she shyly smiles. You seem nice. What's your name?"

"Jerry. What's your name?"

"Jerry, that's an odd name. I am still waiting to hear about it. Jerry, do you think I am pretty."

The rope wraps around the beam a few times and then pulls tight. The other end is now just behind Jerry. The tip starts to flow up.

"Not really. There are a lot of guys with my name. You are more than pretty. You are totally hot."

"Hot?" She looks confused. "I don't understand."

"You must come from a tiny town. You know. Hot. Beautiful. A total babe."

"I understand, beautiful," she said and smiled. The young lady reached up and stroked his face. "I think you want to kiss me. Do you want to kiss me, Jerry?"

"Y-yeah." Jerry stammers. "I mean, who wouldn't."

"Well, you can't!" She yells. "My name is Echo!"

"What?" He gasped as she turned into a hideous, slimy ghoul of a woman. Slime and mud run down her now skeletal form. The rope wrapped around his neck and pulled tight. Then he yanks off his feet up toward the beam."

Echo turns back into the young woman, but now she is wearing a simple white cotton dress that falls to her ankles. She walks over to the computer set and looks at the screen. She seems confused by the computer moving her face even closer. A smile comes to her face when she sees the image of the group standing by the trapdoor.

CHAPTER 14

PECKING ORDER

Carol is standing with the others by the open trapdoor. She nervously looks around. "You just go in and out. Do you hear me, Audrey?"

"Yeah, yeah," Audrey said without looking up as she dropped into the opening. Alex went next, and then Wolsky.

Once they are gone, Carol looks down into the hole and shutters. "One of you stays by the trapdoor. The other is by the front door. I don't care what Audrey says; we are not spending the night here."

"Dibs on the door." Maria quickly said and headed for the front door.

"Oh, come on," Todd said.

"Be a man for once in your life." Carol snaps and hands him the radio. "You stay here and call if anything happens."

"I call while getting my ass out of here." Todd snaps as Carol walks away.

Carol pulls the hood of her poncho up and runs out into the rain. It has lightened up a bit. She runs across to the barn, almost slipping into a puddle. She walks and stops at the sight of the empty chair. "Jerry! Jerry, where the hell are you?"

The young woman walks around and looks at the screen. Everything looks normal. She clicks through the different views. Three times, the screen is filled with static. "Damn, we can't pick up the headcams. Jerry!"

"I don't think Jerry can hear you."

Carol whirls around and stares at Echo. She is back to the young woman in a tee shirt and cutoffs, except now she is completely dry. Her long hair seems to magically float around her face and body. "And you are?"

"Who the hell are you?" Carol growls. "You are trespassing on private property."

"I am not trespassing. You and your friends are trespassing," she said, moving to the middle of the barn. A smile came to her lips. Jerry said you came here looking for ghosts."

"I asked you your name and why are you here."

"Jerry was much more polite. He really liked me, but most men do. I almost had second thoughts, but he tried to kiss me."

"Where is Jerry?" Carol asked. Echo just smiles and nods toward the roof. Her eyes look up. Jerry is hanging from the beam. His body still twitching. His eyes bugled out. His tongue sticking out his lips. Carol looks at Echo, back in ghoul form. Suddenly, she seems to have grown in size, raising her bony fingers over her head. A hideous scream fills the barn. Carol screams and runs out. She stumbles out into the rain, falling in the mud. She crawls along, struggling to get up. A crow dives down and pecks the back of her head. She gasps in pain while touching the back of her head. Here, fingers come back bloody. She pushes herself up onto her knees and looks around.

There are crows everywhere. Their wings flutter. Then, like a black cloud, they launch into the air and swoop at the woman.

Carol screams, trying to bat the crows away. They peck at her clothes, tearing at them. They attack her exposed hands and face. Soon, blood is running down her arms. Crows peck her face. More blood. Her poncho is quickly picked to shears. Carol, now sobbing, struggles against the crows and the rain, trying to get to the house. A large crow swoops in and pecks her eye right out. She screams in horror and clamps a hand over the bloody socket. Now hysterical. Her sobs and screams are as loud as the crow's caws. She stumbles onto the steps. Then, on her hands and knees, she crawls into the house and collapses to the floor.

CHAPTER 15

FIRE AND CREEPY CRAWLERS

"What the hell!" Maria yelled, jumping back as Carol stumbled in and collapsed to the floor. Her whimpering and sobs fill the room. Todd comes running over and rolls her over. Then he jumps back when he sees her bloody face and empty eye socket. Maria gasps. "Where the hell are her eyes?"

"Okay, time to leave," Todd said.

The doors to the house slam shut. The room is suddenly darker. The crows begin to peck at the door. You can hear them flying around the house. Todd jumps up and begins to bang on the door. Maria puts her hands over her ears and screams. Suddenly, it is quiet. A clicking sound comes from the rafters.

Todd keeps banging at the doors, screaming for help. He is so focused on the door that he doesn't notice the first spiders lowering themselves on fine silk lines. These are not your typical house spiders. Their bodies are the size of a tennis ball, shiny black with yellow specks. Long legs fluttered around their body while their giant pincher mouths clicked. The two spiders drop onto Maria's head. Three more crawl down the wall behind her. Maria screams and jumps up, knocking the spiders off. Still crying, she runs across the room. The spiders chase after her while more come down the wall to cut off her escape. She trips on her own feet. The spiders are on her before she can get up.

Only when two spiders crawl down the door does Todd notice them. He jumps back and looks at the small army of spiders crawling walls or coming down on the silk lines. Maria screams, making him look over. She is now covered with spiders. She is rolling around the floor, trying to get the spiders off, but there are too many. "Son of a bitch!"

Maria crawls along. Her pitiful screams and sobs fill the room as she tries to swat the spiders off. They begin to bite her. Blood begins to dribble down her face and arms. Then, boils that look like giant yellow pimples start to appear. The poor woman still tries to crawl away. The spiders crawl over her body and face. She tries to get to her knees. The boils begin to pop. Yellow pus begins to run down her face and arms. Maria finally collapsed into a heap. Her sobs turn to whimpers. Soon, her entire body is covered with spiders. The whimpers stop.

"Hell no!" Todd screams. Then runs for the trapdoor. Just as he gets there, it slams close. He backs up as the spiders move toward him. Suddenly, they stop and back away. Todd nervously laughs until one of the iron claws mounted on the wood rack in the fireplace clamps around his ankle. He screams in agony, falling to the fall. The claw crushes his ankle. The sound of bones breaking fills the room. A huge fireball explodes inside the fireplace. It rolls up the stone mantle, sending a black cloud across the room. Todd tries to pull away, but the claw squeezes his ankle tighter. He screams as the bones are crushed even harder. Blood begins to stream onto the floor. He helplessly paws and hits the metal claw. It starts to pull him closer and closer to the blazing fire. The flames seemed to engulf the entire fireplace. Sweat beads on his forehead. Tears and sweat streamed down his face. Todd frantically tries to pull free. His sneakers begin to smoke and melt. Now, his screams are filled with agony. He rolls over and starts clawing at the floor as he is pulled closer and closer to the impossibly huge flames. His jeans began to smoke. Then flames flare up and run his legs. The next scream is ear-piercing. Todd's is leaving scratches on the floor. His fingertips are now bloody. He looks and stares at the beautiful blonde woman standing before him. Her long cotton dress and hair flow around her body. She kneels down and watches with a passive face. Then she cocks her head to one side and wave bye-bye. "PLEASE HELP ME!"

Echo watches as Todd is pulled to the enormous flames. She watched his flesh quickly turn black. It begins to flake off his body, revealing his skull and bones. The ghost turns away when Todd is nothing more than a charred skeleton. She walks over to Maria. She is unrecognizable. Her whole body was covered with boils, puss, and blood. Echo kneels down and studies the dead body. Then turns and looks toward the trapdoor.

CHAPTER 16

LAST MISTAKE

"Did you hear something?" Wolsky asks, looking back. There is nothing behind him. He can see the light coming from the open trap door. It seems brighter and flickers. "That's not right."

"Come on," Alec said without looking back.

The tunnel has round walls of hard-packed dirt. There are no beams to hold it up. The flat floor is covered with white stones. The ceiling is low, so they have to walk bent over. The only light comes from their flashlights and the trap door.

"Relax, Richard," Alec said, looking back with a grin. "We are going to be just fine.

Audrey says nothing as she moves forward. She suddenly stops. Alex and Wolsky bump into her. She glares at them and points down the tunnel. In the distance is a faint green glow. "Any idea what that is?"

"I have no idea." He pulls out a small meter and points it ahead. "I'm not picking up any EMFs."

Then, the device begins to beep and flash. The arrow on the meter goes flat on the other side. Alec stares at it. "Correction. EMFs are off the scale."

Wolsky blows on his hand. He can see his breath. "It's getting colder. The cold spot is stronger down here."

"Just relax, guys. No one is going to get hurt," Audrey said. I think she knows we are only here to communicate and learn."

The small group moves forward but a little slower. Their breaths fogged out in front of them. They come into a small widening of the tunnel. Audrey comes in and moves her flashlight. She screams when her light beam falls upon a skull. She jumps back but quickly gets a hold of herself. Alex moves beside her and points his light. There is a whole skeleton being held against the wall by thick roots. The bones are bare except for a thick red jacket and leather belt. His jaw is open wide as if he died screaming. Audrey moves the light down to the skeleton's feet. Old, rotten boots are lying by the bones of his feet.

"Who do you think it is?" Wolsky asks, coming up.

"If I didn't know any better," Alex said. "I would say we are looking at the mortal remains of Harry Johnson."

"She kept him down here and let him starve to death?" Wolsky asked.

"He did just vanish. His body was never found." Audrey said, moving closer and studying the open hand. Her light picks up some glittering on the floor. She kneels down and stares down at several gold nuggets. "Gold. She gave him what he wanted. Looks like a small fortune right at his feet."

"Well, he kind of had it coming," Alex said, smiling at Wolsky. I would leave that gold where it is."

"I am greedy, not stupid," Wolsky said. I suppose we should move on."

"That's the plan," Audrey said, giving the skeleton one last look, but now she looked nervous. She glanced and weakly smiled before moving down the tunnel. Their pace was slow and cautious. The tunnel opened up, allowing them to stand. After a couple of steps, all three stopped.

"Good lord." Wolsky gasps.

"I don't think God had anything to do with this," Alex said.

A small room with curved walls and a ceiling has been carved out. Tree roots crisscross the ceiling. The walls and roof are lined with rocks as white as snow. There were strange red symbols painted on the rocks. The floor is one round slab of black rock. A red triangle is painted on it. This is surrounded by even more symbols. In the center of the triangle is a large green crystal. The stone is set into the floor. Several of its thick crystals point toward the ceiling. It gives off a soft glow.

"Any thoughts, gentlemen?" Audrey asked, not stepping into the room.

"Green crystals are usually good," Wolsky said, looking nervous. It is usually the go-to color if you still determine what color crystal will work for you. But I got a bad feeling that isn't good."

"Thank you, professor, for confirming my suggestion that we don't touch the glowing rock," Audrey said. The symbols look a little familiar."

"They could be Celtic, but I don't recognize any of these," Alex said.

"I agree," Wolsky said, poking his head inside. "This was obviously some kind of worship area for Echo and her family."

"Family?" Audrey asked, looking at the professor.

"The small graveyard. Someone was living up here with Echo."

"Excellent point," Audrey said. "What was she worshiping?"

"According to my research, she was known to use herbs and roots for healing purposes," Wolsky said. "Some kind of nature-bound deity. She is very protective of her trees."

"That would fit with Celtic Magic. It would also explain her power over animals." Alec said. "This crystal or whatever it is. Could be why she didn't want people on her hill."

"I am curious where it came from," Audrey said. "Did her family bring it here, or did they find it."

"Those are questions only Echo can answer," Alex said. "I have a feeling she is not good at sharing."

"Maybe. Maybe not." Audrey said. "She let us come down here. Why? I am going in."

"That might not be a good idea," Wolsky said.

"Professor, aside from the crows. She has done nothing harm us. Echo wants to show us something."

"The question is what?" Alec asks.

CHAPTER 29

ECHO'S SECRET

Audrey slowly steps into the room. She wraps her arms around herself and shivers. "Definitely colder here."

Alex looks at his meter. It is still going crazy. He glances at Wolsky. Both look nervous. "Audrey, I am not sure this is a good idea. I have never dealt with anything like this."

Audrey looks over, and for the first time, she seems doubtful. There is an odd sound coming from the walls. She steps back as a green cloud slowly flows up from the crystals. The device in Alex suddenly explodes, sending sparks and smoke into the air. He drops the device. Wolsky turns and runs.

"Richard!" Alex yells, looking back, but the looks back with the sound becomes more apparent. It is a woman weeping. His breathing becomes harder and faster. He begins to shiver as the cloud slowly takes on the form of Echo, a shimmering green specter. Her impossible-long hair floats around her face and body. The long dress flutters around. Her beautiful face becomes clear. A smile slowly spreads across her lips. "Audrey, I think you should get out of there."

Audrey is transfixed by the green specter. She neither moves nor speaks as Echo reaches out and strokes her face. Alex steps in and is about to say something, but Echo turns toward him. The beautiful woman's face turned into a howling green skull with snake-like hair. A bony claw-like hand reaches out for him. Alex screams, falling back into the tunnel. The hideous specter follows him into the tunnel. Another scream and Alex runs down the tunnel without looking back. His panting turns into sobs and then laughter when he sees the trap door. He sees Wolsky climbing up.

Wolsky climbs out the trapdoor and looks back. He sees Alex's fingers grab the edge. Suddenly, the heavy door comes down with a slam. The professor jumped back and gasped. All ten of Alex's bloody stubs are lined up at the trapdoor. He screams, backing up and falling over Todd's burnt skeleton. The black skull's empty sockets stare up at him. Screaming, he crawls away, stopping at the horrible site of Marie's body. Sobbing, he gets to his feet and runs to the door. He glances at Carol, sitting against the door, crying and begging him to help her. Wolsky ignores her, pulling open the door and literally falling out. He pushed it close and leaned against it, trying to catch his breath. Finally, he struggles to his feet, still leaning against the door. A loud growl makes him look at the wolf's head on the door. It jaws open and clamp down on one of his arms. Wolsky screams as he tries to pull free from the jaws. The wolf's head shakes as it chews on the arm.

The man manages to pull free but then realizes the arm has been ripped from his shoulder. He clamps his arm over the bloody wound and staggers away. The blood pours through his fingers and drips to the ground. Wolsky stumbles along, slipping in the mud. Now sobbing, he crawls through the mud. There is a crash of thunder followed by heavy cold rain that seems to push the wounded man down into the mud. The professor slumps. His sobs slowly fade away. He makes one last effort to get up, blood pouring out his mouth and eyes. A mournful sob comes from his lips. Then, his dead body collapses into the mud. The rain suddenly stops.

Echo stands by one of the graves, looking down at it. The muffled sobs and screams of Preston Scott can be heard, along with his fists banging at the coffin lid. His name slowly appears on the black tombstone. Smoke rises from the letters as they appear. After a while, Echo slowly fades away.

PART 2
CHAPTER 1

THE WRITERS

Walt Wilkins sits at his desk, staring at his computer. He doesn't look like a man who writes horror novels. The writer stands just under six feet. His chestnut brown hair is cut short with no grey or loss of hair. This makes the forty-year-old quite happy. He has the same white face as most New Yorkers. Walt is neither handsome nor ugly except for his bright blue eyes. They are the first thing people notice about him. He is stroking the side of his face with two fingers.

Bookcases fill two walls of his study. They are filled with books but not leather-bound editions. Hardbacks, new and old, along with lots of paperbacks, fill these shelves. A colossal TV is mounted on the walls. Around these are shelves filled with various literary awards. The fact they are pretty dusty reflects the man's attitude toward them. His desk is heavy and made of oak. It's an old-fashioned thing made for two people to sit facing each other. Behind his computer monitor is another monitor, along with a keyboard. Walt sits in a red and black gaming chair. The chair across is also a gaming chair but yellow and purple.

Colleen Wilkins walks into the room, an attractive blonde in her mid-thirties. Her long hair is pulled up into a messy bun held together with a pencil. The oversized red sweater hanging loose on her slender frame leaves one shoulder bare. Black yoga pants and pink bunny slippers complete her fashion statement. Her face is kinder than beautiful, and she has small laugh lines around her hazel eyes. She smiles, which lights up her whole face. "Still trying to figure out how to kill the head vampire?"

"I had an idea for a stake made out of holy water," Walt said, looking at his wife. Then I remembered Watershaw already did that."

"In his book and real life," Colleen said, sitting across from him. She put her bunny slippers on top of the desk and leaned back.

"Don't remind me. Waterhaw still in Los Angeles...No Venice Beach."

"Isn't he dating that actress who starred in the movies based on his books?"

"If you believe the tabloids. Yes, he is. You know those bunny slippers always get me turned on."

"You are a sick man...but since I wear them. What does that make me?"

"So incredibly sexy. Maybe I will buy you some bunny ears."

"Okay, now you're moving onto really strange...which I like," Collen said with a smile. We could quit early, order Chinese food, and watch a movie. You might get lucky."

"Tease."

"Pervert."

Walt's phone roars like Godzilla. He snatches it up and looks at the face. "We got trouble."

"Echo Hill?"

"What else. Let's hope the lady just said boo." Walt said, tapping the face of his phone. "Hello, sheriff, give me the bad news."

"You don't know him, but Heath just crawled out of the river, almost drowned, and was a little crazy. Doc says he will live. But he was the only one to come back down. I'm putting together a search party to go up. We will start the hike in the morning."

"I don't want you hiking up there, sheriff," Walt said, looking at his wife and shaking her head. I will arrange for a couple of helicopters."

"I think we will only need one...wait. You're thinking bodies."

"Let me know what you find, and let's keep this quiet for now. If Audrey Lang is dead. Her father will be looking for someone to blame."

"I hear you."

"Don't worry, sheriff. He will probably come after me. Oh, you know not to stay up at night."

"Yeah, you don't have to tell me that."

CHAPTER 2

FINDING THE DEAD

A helicopter comes down and hovers about the clearing beside the logging camp. The pilot is being careful not to touch the ground. He looks around nervously. Sheriff Royal jumps out. Two deputies, a young paramedic and a man in a suit and tie, follow him. One of the deputies helps a dog out and pats its head. They all run away from the chopper. It flies up and hovers. Royal touches the mike on his shoulder. "You take a few turns around the hill. Let me know if you spot anything. Then head home. I will call you when needed."

"Are you sure that is wise?" the man in the suit asked, pulling his coat tighter. Mr. Lang wants a thorough search."

"Mr. Benning, you are here as a courtesy," Royal said, looking at the man and shaking his head. I told you to get some boots and a jacket. Come on. Let's get this done."

Adam takes the lead but stops by the unfinished mill. He glances at the waterwheel. It slowly turns. The sheriff kneels down, picks up some shells, and jingles them in his hand, looking at the dead bear. "Heath did say it was a damn big bear, and that is a big bear."

"Biggest one I ever seen," one of the deputies said. I don't think I have seen one that black, either.

"Let go," Royal said. I don't want to be here any longer than necessary."

The group moves up the trail, stopping to look at the dried mud. The dog begins to sniff the ground, and then the deputy pulls along.

"Is that a cadaver dog?" The man in the suit asked.

"No, just the best hunting dog in the county." The sheriff said. "This looks like a mudslide, but the ground is flat. Come on."

The dog and deputy reach the edge of a slope. The dog starts to back. The deputy looks down, spotting Earl's dead body still impaled on the tree. "We found Earl."

The group runs up and looks down. Adam looks at the paramedic. "You want to go down and check him."

"No, he most certainly dead." The paramedic said. "Odd. No animals have gotten to him."

"Yeah, that's odd. We'll need search and rescue to get him up. I'll call while we walk."

A short time later, the group approaches the house and barn. Adam stops them, telling them to wait. He slowly moves up the path, stopping by the body of Richard Wolsky. It is covered with dried mud, leaves, and blood. He notes the missing arm. "Damn. We got another body."

Everyone moves up and looks down at the body. The dog barks while the deputy looks around.

"It looks like his arm was ripped out of the sockets. I can't be sure because of the mud, but it looks like a big animal did it. Anyone see the arm?"

"Yeah, over on the porch," the deputy said. "Right under that wolf's head."

"Are you suggesting that wood wolf bit this man's arm off?" The lawyer asked.

"Not saying anything. Just pointing out where the arm is." The deputy says

"We'll take a quick peek in the barn and then look in the house," the sheriff said. We better call the chopper. I assume we have more bodies.

"We going call the state police." The other deputy asks.

"Yup, we don't have the people or facilities to deal with this," Royal said, walking over to the barn. "Let's see how many we got."

They all walk over to the barn and look inside. The computer and all their gear are still there. The sheriff walks up and looks it over. "Well, all their equipment is here. It looks like they have cameras set up in the house. It's too dark to see anything."

The dog barks, pulling at the leash. The deputy looks around and then up. Jerry's body is still hanging from the rafter. "Sheriff, we got another one. How the hell did he get up there?"

"Obviously, the young man hung himself for some reason. Nothing supernatural about that." The lawyer said smugly.

"You see ladder around here?" the sheriff asked and walked off before he could get an answer. The deputies and paramedics followed. The lawyer looked up at the body but realized he was alone and chased after them.

"All right, let's all be careful," Royal said, looking down at the arm and the wolf's head. He touched the fangs and then rubbed his fingers together. "We got three dead bodies. Let's hope there aren't more."

Adam pulls open the doors and steps in. He takes a deep breath before walking inside. The first thing the sheriff sees is the two dead bodies, and quickly moves toward them. He stops by Maria's. Her face and body are still covered with boils, pus, and blood. She barely looks human. A look of disgust and horror fills his face. The group comes up and stares down. One of the deputies starts to gag. Royal glares at him. "Take it outside."

The deputy runs out the open doors. The sheriff looks over at the burnt skeleton. "What the hell happened here?"

The dog sniffs and keeps trying to pull away from the deputy. Finally, he follows the dog over. It begins to sniff at the fingers. The deputy looks over and screams. "Son of bitch! We got fingers over here."

The deputy manages to pull the dog away before he eats one. The sheriff, lawyer, and paramedic came over and stared down at the bloody stumps. Royal kneels down and studies the floor. "Looks like we got some kind of trap door here."

The deputy who threw up comes back and wipes his mouth. A soft moaning makes her look over. He sees Carol's curled-up body in the corner. The deputy goes over and kneels down. He touches her shoulder. Carol looks up and whimpers. "Help me, please help me."

The deputy fell back, horrified by her bloody face and missing eyes. He looks back and yells. "WE GOT A LIVE ONE!"

CHAPTER 3

THE POWER OF WEALTH

Robert Lang not only had billions of dollars but also looked like a billionaire. He was well over six feet tall, wearing a gray suit tailored to his slender frame. His face is tanned yet lined with wrinkles, giving him the look of someone who demands respect. His silver hair is trimmed by a hairstylist. Grey eyes that had no warmth were the center of his face. He stands in an office in one of New York's tallest buildings. The décor of the office is modern and efficient. There is no warmth to it. There are no personal items on the glass-top desk. Just a laptop and neat piles of documents. He strokes the large gold ring on his right finger. It is the only piece of jewelry he wears. On his wrist is the cheap Timex given to him by his grandfather. It was supposed to remind him that Granddad started with nothing. He stares out over the city. "So they haven't found my daughter's body?"

"No sir," A young man in a black suit said. He is a clean-cut fellow with wire-rimmed glasses. Blake Allen looks like he would rather be anywhere but here. "They found most of the bodies. Audrey, along with two others, is still missing. Professor Wagner's fingertips were found by a trap door, but they couldn't seem to get it open."

"Then chop the thing open or just blow it to hell." Lang snaps.

"They tried that, sir. It didn't work. They tried digging down to where they supposed the tunnel to be, but all they had at this time was a deep hole. The locals will only go up during the day. It is impossible to get heavy equipment up there. Something to do with the winds..."

"You are trying to tell me there actually is some truth to the legend of this Echo Hill."

"Sir, I am just reporting what I know is being done."

Lang turns and studies the floor, and then Blake. "Tell me about these writers."

"They write horror novels and are quite successful. They are rich but not on your level. They bought Echo Hill from the town for nothing, what it is worth. The town was always getting sued because people kept going up there. Most of them died, but some just vanished. They have gone to great lengths to keep people off of it. Your daughter was trespassing, so any legal action..."

"I am not going to sue them. They used to do this ghost hunting?"

"Oh yes, they were and still are quite respected in the paranormal community. They occasionally give lectures and advise others on their research but are no longer...hunted ghosts. They stay in New York except when they do signings or go on vacation."

"They stopped after Echo Hill?"

"Yes, according to all reports, they barely got back alive. They knew the danger and left their team at the mountain's base. Only Walt and his wife went up. They were up there for less than four hours, but it took weeks for them to fully recover. Not just physically but emotionally. There is some video, but it is so grainy it is hard to tell what really happened. "

"But they got back alive?"

"Yes."

"That's who I need to go up," Lang said, walking behind his desk. "If anyone can find my daughter, it will be them. Make them an offer."

"Sir, as I told you, they are already rich," Blake meekly said. They have given us full access to the mountain. They have been more than cooperative, even making suggestions to the searchers."

"We need them up there," Lang growls. He looks annoyed. This is a man who always gets what he wants. "We can't waste time in court. Call legal and find me something. Wait, the man who managed to survive."

"Two survived. A man and woman. Both are lucky to be alive. The woman is in intensive care. She will recover physically in time. But mentally and emotionally..."

"The man is in good shape. Have him arrested for murder. There is another way to get this couple to come around to my way of thinking."

"Want would that be?" Blake asked.

"Something my daughter stumbled across. It was one of the reasons she went up there."

CHAPTER 4

I HAVE A PLAN

"I can't believe they arrested that young man for murder," Colleen said, pacing around the room but stopping to watch her husband. He is slumped back in his office chair. His hand is extended out in front of him. A pen is slowly spinning over his fingers. It goes up and down. It floats across the room. Colleen snatches out of the air. "Fine-tuning your powers? You better. Spinning a pen isn't going to cut it."

"I thought spinning film reels and exploding computers, and lights would have scared them," Walt said, looking over as he put both hands out and closed his eyes. Several things in the office slowly float and then gently come back down. He sits up and smiles.

"Now you are just showing off."

"Well, we are going to need my talents. I'm figuring out what Lang's game is. He gets that man arrested and then holds a press conference telling the world he is a direct descendant of Harry Jackson."

"Do you think he is?" Colleen asked.

"I don't know. Don't care. If Lang wants that damn mountain. He can have it. As you know, my dear, I can't read minds, but if I can get close enough, I could pick up his real motive. Is he motivated by genuine loss or just a need for closure? I don't think it is love."

"How can you be sure? It isn't love?"

"I don't need psychic powers to know that. Lang is still here in New York. His daughter is missing in Oregon. If he cared that much, he would be in Oregon. Up on Echo Hill leading the search, but he isn't."

"Maybe he is going through the motions to protect his image. He is the figurehead of a worldwide corporate empire."

"About that, Thomas advised us to take our money out of his companies last year. He may not be as rich as people think. Like our president. It could be yelling mixed with smoke and mirrors."

'It would help to know if he was actually afraid of Echo Hill."

"That's it. We show that Lang is actually afraid of Echo Hill. All that he is doing is to get us to go up there. Then, he can declare to the world that he has done everything possible to find his daughter. Even getting the two people who came down alive. But it could backfire. It could end up with us going back up. But this time, we have to be prepared. We will not be going up there to do research. Our goal this time will be to get back down alive."

"And how do we do that?"

"I have some ideas. I am sure you do, too. Are you still friends with that Celtic Witch Coven?

"Yes, I see where you are going."

"We will need to know how she killed all those people to start with. Do some research? Contact a few old friends. But first a press conference."

CHAPTER 5

THE CHALLENGE

A large room is packed with reporters and cameramen. A stage with a podium is set up. Everyone is talking but stops when Walt and Colleen walk up to the stage. A few reporters yell questions, but they are ignored. Walt moves behind the podium and waits for the crowd to quiet down. He unconsciously pulls at the collar of the shirt he is wearing. He looks out of place in a suit. Collen is wearing a simple black dress.

"Ladies and Gentlemen, thanks for coming," Walt said with a nervous smile. "I am not used to speaking in public, so excuse me if I stutter. We all know why we are here. Audrey Lang, Preston Scott, and Alec Wagner are still missing. I would like to point out I knew Alex and respected him. Certain parties have insisted my wife and I go up Echo Hill to aid in the search. People seemed to be thinking since we have been up there. We could be of help."

"Are you saying you can't be of help?" One of the reporters yells.

"Another yells. "It is rumored that Robert Lang has hired renowned psychic Aramis Bouvier to help in the search?"

"I have heard that too. I know of Mr. Bouvier and his reputation." Walt said, almost rolling his eyes, but stopped himself. "I did use to do some paranormal research. Did is the keyword in that sentence. We are now writers."

"That's not really true. I hear you still do research."

"We dabble in it but are not active in it. We are more consults and lecturers now. If Miss Lang had come to us, I would have warned that Echo Hill is a dangerous place and not go there. We getting off track. Her father has recently claimed to be a direct descendant of Harry Johnson. By now, you all know who it was. Is Mr. Lang a direct descendent? I have no idea. But if he is. Echo Hill is the last place he would want to go. Echo Hacker would be thrilled to have him there."

"You are talking like she is real?" A lady reporter yelled and laughed.

"I thought I made myself perfectly clear. Echo Hacker is real and very dangerous. How many bodies do you need to prove that?"

"Heath Miller has been arrested for those murders." She retorts.

"Arrested, yes, but he will never be convicted. The evidence will show it would have been impossible for Mr. Miller to commit those murders. One of the victims was his brother. I am sure she will clear the man once Carol Holtz can do this. Once again, I am here to make a statement. No challenge to Mr. Lang."

"Challenge?" Someone asked.

"We will return to Echo Hill, but we have conditions," Walt said grimly. One, Heath Miller, will be immediately released, and all charges will be dropped. Two, Mr. Lang will sign a document provided by his attorneys stating he has no legal claim to Echo Hill. We take a small team up. A helicopter will take us up to the site at dawn. We remain there until we discover what happened to Audrey Lang or the sun sets."

"Will that help?" The lady reporter asked. "Rumors suggest all the murders happen during the day?"

"Well, as the man said. It can't hurt to be careful. The team will be my wife and me. A representative of whatever law enforcement has jurisdiction, a guide whom we trust, and Mr. Bouvier is welcome, but I doubt he will join us. Lastly, Mr. Robert Lang will join us."

The room explodes with gasps and yelling. Walt waits for things to calm down. "Mr. Lang insists there is no danger up there. Yet he is safely here in New York and not in Oregon. Lang sent out representatives, but it was all phone calls and press conferences. He can even bring a bodyguard along, but that person will be of little help. Those are my terms. Mr. Lang, I await your answer. The clock is ticking."

CHAPTER 6

THE RESPONSE
"You bastard."

CHAPTER 7

GEARING UP

In jeans and a sweatshirt, Collen walks into a small gun store. She glances at the weapons. A large man in a red flannel shirt waits behind the counter. A smile appears under his bushy beard. "Colleen, I haven't seen you out at the range. You've got to keep practicing."

"Walt insists I go this afternoon," Colleen said before hugging the man and stepping back. "How are you, bro? Were you able to do it?"

"Yeah, no big deal." He said, looking around to make sure the store was empty. "I made four. The detonator is small. Don't even be close to them when they go."

"I don't plan on being near them," Colleen said. "How much?"

"Like I am going to charge my sister. Just be careful. You parked out front? I'll carry them out for you."

"This was an interesting problem." An old man in a lab coat said. It is not only the lab coat that makes him look like a scientist. The white curls, beak nose, and black-framed glasses add to the image. Walt and the man are standing in what looks like a chemistry lab. "Getting the mixture right was simple. The hard part was the detonation. The boys over in engineer came up with a fob. Works just like a fob for your car. Press the button and boom."

"Will it be harmful?" Walt asks.

"Not to humans." The scientist laughs at his own joke. Walt is not amused.

An older woman with red hair comes from the backroom to a store specializing in gifts and cards. Most of the products are Irish-influenced. She wears a white blouse, black jeans, and several silver chains with pendants. The lady smiles and hugs Colleen. Then, she steps out and looks her friend over. "You look well," she says.

"Thank you," Collen said. "So do you...is it ready?"

"We have been at all night."

"Really?" Colleen asks, now interested.

"The construction was simple, and we knew most symbols. The hard part was putting the charms and spells on it. Listen, Collen, I don't know how much protection this will give you. It may just stall her for only a few minutes."

"Actually, that's what we are hoping. If it lasts longer. Great."

"We will hold a circle for you while you are there."

"We appreciate that. Well, show me."

"Theoretically, these should work." An old man said, sitting across a table in a cozy kitchen. He actually looks ancient. His dark, wrinkled skin and long gray hair reflect his Native American heritage. A small pendant made of turquoise silver hangs around his neck. He held up a small leather pouch about the size of a ping-pong ball. "Just pull the string and throw. It won't kill her but will give you time to run."

"Abe, I am seeing a lot of running in my future," Walt said.

"This man, Lang," Abe said, leaning forward. "Don't trust him. A man who acquires that kind of wealth and power is not to be trusted. When the danger comes. He will run and not care what happens to you."

"Actually, I count on him to be a coward. We may not have to go all the way."

"I will pray for you."

"We will need it."

"Walt, we both know you were lucky last time. This time, she will be ready for you."

"You give a hell of a pep talk, you know that.

Colleen parks her car in front of a salvage yard. She gets out and looks around. She walks to the gate only after she is sure no one is around. The lock is undone. She closed the gate behind her, approached the back, came around a corner, and stopped. Walt is standing in an open area. Three junked cars are slowly rotated about him. He makes slow circles. Slowly, the cars come to rest. He turns and smiles.

"That's most you have lifted in a while," Colleen said. "How do you feel?"

"Good, I don't feel like I just ran a marathon," Walt said. "No headache or nose bleeds. I may be stronger."

"Let's hope so. Lang is trying to pull something."

"What makes you say that?"

"Heath is out of jail, but Lang wants him to be our guide. In his words, the young man is experienced."

"How does Heath feel all about this?"

"He said he will go but insists we talk first."

"We got everything, so let's fly out tonight. Where's Lang?"

"Still here. What happens if Lang doesn't show up?"

"We don't go. Lang needs to go. We don't dare go without him. I mean, he is our bait."

CHAPTER 8

A CALM BEFORE THE GHOST

The sun slowly rose over the far-off mountains. The shadowy landscape is gradually revealed as the sun rises into the sky. A blue sky with no clouds in sight. A small airport with a wood control tower sits at the edge of a clearing. It is surrounded by trees. There is a short runway and two landing pads. This place caters to helicopters and small prop planes. At this time, only one chopper is sitting on one of the pads. It is an older helicopter painted white with a red strip on the side.

Walt and Heath, both dressed in jeans and flannel shirts, are checking three large backpacks sitting on the grass. In jeans and a red sweatshirt, Colleen paces around as she talks on the phone. The pilot is checking the chopper while occasionally looking over. He doesn't look happy.

"These are nice axes," Heath said. "I may keep one."

"You are welcome to both, but you may not have time to grab them," Walt said with a smile. Are you clear on the plan?"

"Let's hope it works," Heath said. "It would be nice to get some payback."

"Heath, we can't kill or make her disappear in another dimension or plane. She is here because she wants to be here. Protecting her home. We are just here to maybe find some bodies. But something in my head tells me Audrey Lang is still alive."

"After all this time? Why would she kill the rest and leave Audrey alive?"

"I think we see the reason coming now," Walt says, nodding toward the SUV pulling up. Lang, two men, and a woman climb out and walk toward them. Lang is dressed in top-of-the-line jeans, a shirt, a vest, and a baseball cap, all looking new.

The woman is dressed in black jeans, a turtleneck, and boots. Her bright red leather jacket is fur-lined with a hood. She is a tall, slender woman with short red curls. His oval face seems to lack any sign of emotion or concern. Her thin lips are tight lines. She takes off her sunglasses, revealing hazel eyes that are quite beautiful. Even from this distance, they can see she is studying them. The slightest smile comes to her lips. It softens her face for a moment. She starts to follow Lang. Her walk and confidence scream professional. The wind makes her jacket fly up, revealing a hip holster holding a pistol. Gillian Clay quickly pushes her jacket down over her pistol but seems unconcerned that everyone has seen it. Once again, she smiles.

One of the men is wearing a tanned uniform with a Mountie-style hat. He wears the uniform with an attitude of self-importance. He is slender but has a softness and lack of self-confidence that is apparent. He keeps making sure his pistol is still in his holsters. Gillian seems to be amused by this. The officer has a round face and black-framed glasses, making him look more like a librarian or teacher than a state trooper. There is a gold chain with a cross around Cole Wayne's neck. A pocket on his shirt bugles from the small bible he keeps there. He is carrying a jacket that matches his green uniform.

The last man is wearing jeans and a black shirt covered with the twelve Astrological symbols. A silver chain around his neck holds the Isis symbol's giant eye. The outfit must be corrected for a mountain, especially the street shoes. Dr. Aramis Bouvier walks with his chin and nose up, looking like a man who knows he is better than anyone around him. He has a leather shoulder bag over one shoulder. He stops, closes his eyes, and raises his hands.

"It looks like everything Mr. Lang is wearing is brand spanking new," Heath said. He is lucky we aren't hiking much. New boots mean blisters. Who is the lady with the gun?"

"His bodyguard, I would guess. I would say she knows how to use it. I will have to ask Colleen. She loves to shoot," Walt said, studying the group. He smiled and looked up when Colleen put away her phone and kneeled by the two men. "News?"

"Our friend at the airport overheard Mr. Lang telling his pilot to be ready to take off at moment's notice," Collen said. "He got the impression Lang doesn't plan on being here long."

"What is he up to?" Heath asked. "I got the impression Audrey wasn't close to her dad."

Walt studies Lang and finally says. "Something about money. I promise you that."

The small group walks up. Lang introduces them to Cole and Gillian. Bouvier walks with a big smile on his face. "I am picking up excellent vibes here. Everyone's aura looks quite positive."

Heath smiles. Then looks at the shiny black shoes. "Nice shoes. Pity if they get ruined."

"I was told it really wouldn't be much of a hike. The compound appears mostly flat." He said with a haughty tone.

"You are right," Colleen said. "But they will be crabby for running."

"Let's get on with this," Lang snaps and walks away. Bouvier follows. Gillian stands there for a moment. A small smile comes, and then a shake of the head. Another look and she is gone. The pilot looks over, shakes his head, and reluctantly climbs into the chopper.

"I want to make one thing clear," Cole said, putting his hands on his hips and trying to look taller than he was. "I don't believe all this mumbo jumbo about ghosts and voodoo. I am a born-again Christian and deacon at my church. What I do believe is that the man there killed all those people. I plan to prove it."

"That's why you volunteered?" "Walt asked.

"How do you know I volunteered?" Cole asked, looking surprised.

"Oh, you just look like the volunteering type." Walt smiled as he picked up one of the heavy packs. Heath and Colleen picked up theirs, and they moved toward the chopper.

"That is a lot of gear for just one day." The officer said, following them.

"Girl Scout," Colleen said with a smile. "Always be prepared."

"That's Boy Scouts."

"You saying a woman can't be prepared? Yikes!" Collen said with a surprised look.

"This is not the time for jokes."

"I have to make my jokes now," Colleen said, putting her pack onto the chopper. "Once we are up there. There won't be time for jokes. I like your cross. Oh, we are not into Voodoo. We practice a completely different mumbo jumbo."

Cole puts his hand over the cross on his chest. Then he looks up toward the mountain. Heath climbs in, leans out, and smiles. "Are you coming or not, officer?"

"Of course," Cole snaps but rubs his cross before climbing onto the helicopter.

CHAPTER 9

NO BACKING OUT NOW

The helicopter descends into the logging camp and lands. Everyone but Lang and Gillian climb out. Walt looks back and smiles. Gillian has her pistol pointed at them, but she is not smiling or threatening. It seems like she knows something. Lang smiles. "My associate and I will be returning to base. You will call when you find my daughter's body."

"It's never easy," Walt said with a sign. Heath steps toward the chopper, but Gillian coolly smiles, taking aim. Suddenly, the pistol flies out of her hand and lands at Colleen's feet. Then Gillian flies out and lands on the ground with a thud. Heath grabs Lang by his shirt and pulls him out. Then, he drags him toward a tree and slams him against it. Cole goes for his pistol, but Walt looks at him and says in a cold voice. "Don't."

Gillian scrambles for the pistol, but Colleen snatches it up and fires two shots into the ground a couple inches from the woman's face. "I belong to the New York Shooting Club. My ex-marine brother taught me how to shoot."

Gillian pushes herself to her knees and raises her hands. A cold smile comes to her lips. "I knew it. From the moment I saw you, I knew you were someone to not underestimate."

"You coming or what?" The pilot yells. "I want to get out of here."

"I am flattered," Collen said, walking over to where Heath held Lang. Walt walked up, and so did Bouvier, who looked outraged.

"Was all this violence necessary?" He asked.

"Hey, he started it," Walt said, smiling beside Lang. "Okay, Lang, I will make it easy. We all get on the chopper, or no one gets on the chopper. "So, do we stay or go?"

"Answer the man." Heath snarled.

"This is getting out of hand." Cole snapped once again, going for his gun. Walt looks back. The officer struggles with his pistol. It won't come out of his holster. Gillian watches this with an amused smile and cocked eyebrow. Then looks back at Walt. That small smile again.

"Welcome to Echo Hill, Officer Wayne. So what's going to be Lang?"

Lang looks pissed. After a long moment, he mutters. "We are staying."

"I would ask why, but you won't tell me," Walt said, tapping Heath on the shoulder. Heath lets Lang go. Cole falls back on his butt when he finally gets his pistol out. He stares at the gun and then up at Walt. "Let's get our gear and move on."

"About time." The pilots yell as they pull out the gear.

Once the gear is out. The group watches the chopper fly off. Colleen hands the pistol back to Gillian with a smile. "You can shoot me now if you want."

"I'll wait," Gillian said with a smile. "You might still be useful. I've been to places. Seen things. So, contrary to what our friendly neighborhood officer believes. I think there is something to your...mumbo jumbo."

"I apologize."

"For what."

"I thought you were one of those macho types that thinks a gun can solve most problems. You are so more than that."

"So you underestimated me. So we are even."

"I'm starting to like you," Colleen smiles and walks away, joining Heath and Walt by the packs. "So we go with Plan B."

"Plan B," Walt said, looking at Lang. "I don't get it. I was sure he was going to chicken out."

"The man was afraid," Heath said, looking in the same direction. "Still is."

Bouvier walks over and points down the trail. "So the house is this way?"

"Yeah, about a half hour," Walt said. He looked at the shirt and necklace. They were beautiful. Did you bring a jacket?"

"A little hot for a jacket." The psychic said.

"It is now. I thought you would have seen the need to bring a jacket," Walt said and walked away. "Of course, I am not psychic on reality shows."

"Hey, I have awards!"

Walt slings on his backpack smiles, and starts up the trail. Heath follows. Colleen walks by and pats his shoulder. "I like your show. It's always makes me laugh."

"It's not a comedy. It is a serious show about my powers and the paranormal."

"My bad," Colleen said without looking back. "I thought it was a comedy.

CHAPTER 10

MUMBO JUMBO STUFF

Walt, Heath, and Colleen reach the compound first. They stopped just down from the house and barn. It all looks so peaceful.

"I don't get it," Heath said. "No crows."

"Yes, I noticed that, too," Walt said. I hope it stays that way. We couldn't figure out how to fight a bunch of crows."

"That is a murder of crows, dear," Colleen said.

"Thanks for reminding me," Walt said. Bouvier comes and pushes past Walt. Walt stops him with his hands on his chest. "Stop."

"Yes, yes, I can feel an evil presence here," Bouvier said, putting his fingers on his forehead. "We must be careful. Very careful."

"Thanks for the heads up," Walt said dryly. "Put your hand out."

"What?"

"Put your hand out," Walt speaks slowly like he talking to a child.

Confused, The psychic sticks out his hands, gasps, and pulls them back. "Oh my god, a cold spot. A real cold spot."

"The whole compound is a cold spot. Welcome to Echo Hill," Walt said, turning and looking back at the group. From his point of view, it gets really dangerous. It's still time to call the chopper."

"I didn't come this far to go back," Lang growls, moving past Walt. He takes two steps and gasps. "Geez, it's freezing."

"I should have brought a jacket," Walt said, moving forward. Colleen and Heath followed, and then the rest of the party reluctantly followed. Cole pulled on the jacket he was holding.

"My God, there it is," Bouvier said, moving toward the house. Once again, Walt stopped him.

"Barn first. Then house. We got things to do first."

"What things?" Bouvier asks.

"You don't know?" Walt said, walking toward the barn. Heath follows. Colleen comes up by the psychic. Once she pats his shoulder.

"He's just joking. My husband makes jokes when he is in a stressful situation."

"He is stressed?"

"Aren't you?" She asked and walked off.

Walt comes in and glances at the computer setup. He takes off his jacket and puts it down. "They didn't take the computers?"

"They took the drives," Cole said. "We couldn't find any cameras. We hoped they would show what the gentlemen did to those people."

"Maybe there weren't any cameras?" Bouvier said, wrapping his arms around his shoulders. Walt opened his pack and pulled out two thick sweatshirts. He tossed them to Lang and Bouv

ier.

"See," Colleen said, putting down her pack. "Girl scouts."

"A reality show without cameras? I don't think so." Walt said, moving to the center of the barn and glancing up at the beam where Jerry had been hanging. "We will set up here."

"Set up what?" Lang asked.

"You dragged us up here because you thought we were experts," Colleen said. We are. Let's set up, and we may all go home."

Heath, Colleen, and Walt start taking stuff out of their packs. Three vests with multiple pockets, a folded leather tarp, and several canisters. Some red. Others white. Two with the image of a spider on the side. Walt unfolds the round tarp. It is a good-sized thing with a green circle almost covering the surface. Inside are various odd symbols and runes. He smooths it out. He gets a hammer and steel stakes from his pack. "I'll stake it down. Heath, start making the trench."

"Right," Heath said, getting a small folding shovel from his pack. He started to dig a small trench around the tarp.

Gillian walks over, fascinated. She kneels down and picks up one of the canisters. With another smile, she puts it down. "Is there Anything I can do to help?"

"Yes, if you could put a white canister in the left stall and a red canister in the right. That would be wonderful." Jennifer said.

Gillian nods and picks up one of each canister.

"What is all this?" Bouvier seems really interested.

"A waste of time," Lang growls. "We should search the house now."

"You are more welcome to go into the house and search," Walt said without looking up as he pounded stakes through the tarp into the ground.

"Sir, it might be wise to wait." Gillian quietly said. "I mean, this is their field of expertise."

She saunters back toward the stalls.

"I am not comfortable with all this mambo jumbo stuff." Cole snaps. "Looks like voodoo junk."

"Actually, it's Celtic and Native American magic with some science thrown in," Colleen said, putting a white canister on one side of the entrance and a red one on the other. Two other white canisters are placed around the very edge of the tarp. "But please go investigate. We will join you shortly."

Cole snorts, walks toward the door, and stops at the entrance because now he can see his breath. He notices several crows perched in the trees but none in the compound. The deputy stares at the house. His hand drops to his pistol when, for a brief second, he sees the image of a young woman in one of the windows. He stares, but she is gone. "Sun playing with my eyes."

"Done," Heath said, finishing his trench. He dropped the shovel and pulled out a small but heavy burlap sack. "Pour?"

"Pour," Walt said, checking his stakes.

Heath opens the sack and fills the trench with what looks like salt.

"Is that salt?" Gillian asks after coming back. "I saw a TV where they used salt as protection from ghosts."

"You see, TV can be educational," Colleen said. Walt doesn't think so, but he watches much of it."

"Research." He mutters, checking on Heath.

"It is salt mixed with several other things like herbs. The tarp was made by some Celtic witches. Then they put some charms and spells on it. When all hell breaks loose. Run here. It may be our only chance of survival."

"When?" The bodyguard asks.

"Walt and I have been here before. Things are going to happen very quickly. Stay on your toes."

"Thanks for the heads up."

"If we get out of her alive. You would make a great character in one of our books."

"Let's get off this hill first," Gillian said with a smile, looking slightly flattered.

"Right," Collen said, going over and stepping into the middle of the circle. Heath stands up and nods. She pulls out a piece of paper from her pocket and poses solemnly. "Who will hold my hand? Who will send the energy on to weave a circle of light? I call on the light, I call to the Lord and the Lady, whatever you wish to call them, I call to the four corners of the Earth, Strengthen this circle and let the power grow, Let the love flow!"

"Well, we are as ready as we will be," Walt said. He turns to Heath. "Get the axes."

CHAPTER 11

AXES, FIRE, AND POISON

The group comes out of the barn and heads toward the house. Once again, Bouvier tries to move ahead. Once again, Walt stops him. "Last time. Next time, I will let you walk into it."

"What is your problem with me?" Bouvier snaps. "Is because I understand this place better than you do. I have powers you will never understand."

"The only power you have is to con people out of their money. To me, you are nothing more than a snake oil salesman," Walt said coolly. "You want to go into that house? Go into it. Me, I am going over to that graveyard."

Walt, Heath, and Colleen walk toward the small graveyard. Lang stands still but finally moves. Gillian follows, followed by the last two.

Walt comes to the small fence and looks at the graves. He looks at Heath. "What was the name of that psychic who came up here?"

"Ah, Scott. Preston Scott." Heath said.

"Oh, that man was a complete fraud," Bouveir snaps. He never should have been up here. Why do you ask?"

"Check out the name on that tombstone in the back," Walt said.

"Oh my God!" The psychic gasps. "He's buried there! Why would she bury him?"

"Maybe she doesn't like psychics?" Colleen asks.

"Nervous," Walt asked. "I think he was alive. She put him down there."

"Stop it," Cole said, sounding authoritative. We have no way of knowing the man is down there."

"Sure there is. Dig up the grave. Want to borrow our shovel?"

"I will make a note of it. We will have to check, but not right now." Cole said, pulling out a small notebook and pen.

"Wolf's head," Walt said, heading toward the house. Heath followed. Collen gathered wood and piled it a few yards before the house.

The rest of the group follow and watch as Walt and Heath stand on both sides of the wolf's head.

"We are not going in?" Lang asks.

"Not yet, sir," Colleen said, walking toward the barn.

"You can go in," Walt said. "I'll hold the door for you."

"I will wait. There may be a method to your madness." Lang mutters.

Walt and Heath start to chop the wolf's head off the door. It splinters and breaks. Falling in pieces onto the porch. One of the red eyes pops out. It looks like a giant ruby. Bouvier reaches out to pick it up. "Don't touch that!"

Bouvier pulls back his hand. Walt brings down the blunt end of the ax on the jewel, shattering it into pieces. He does the same with the other eye.

"Those could have been worth a fortune." The psychic gasped.

"Maybe, but not caring," Walt said, returning to chopping the last of the head.

Colleen comes back with the two canisters with spider images on them. She is also carrying a can of lighter fluid for a barbeque. Gillian walks over and watches her pour lighter fluid over the wood pile. "I thought you were Girl Scout. No rubbing sticks together."

"I miss that class," Colleen said, pulling out a book of matches and lighting one. She sets the whole book on fire and drops it onto the stick. She jumps back as a tiny fireball explodes upwards. "Besides, I like watching the fireball."

"Me too."

Walt and Heath had chopped off the wolf's head, careful not to make a hole in the door. They begin to gather up the pieces. Then, carry them over to Colleen's blazing fire. They throw the pieces into the fire and watch them burn. Walt looks up at the crows and sighs.

"Now, can we go in?" Bouvier asked.

"I made it clear you can go in any time you want," Walt said, taking one of the canisters from Colleen. He, Heath, and Colleen climbed onto the porch. Heath grabbed one door handle. Walt and Colleen put their fingers on rings mounted into the tops of the canisters. "Anyone going in? Last chance?"

No one moves.

Walt and Colleen nod. Heath opens the door just enough for them to throw the canisters in. They pull the rings and toss them inside the house. There is a pop followed by a hissing sound. Heath slams the door shut.

"What was that?" Bouvier asked.

"It's the most powerful bug bomb we could find," Walt said, coming down. It kills everything, especially spiders. Now we wait."

"For how long?" Lang asked.

"About an hour. Then we open the windows and doors. Another half hour to clear out the poison. So we should be in there well before ten. If lucky, we will be home for lunch or dead."

"What do we do in the meantime?" Bouvier asked.

"Well, I don't know about you, but I am going to have a cup of coffee and a Kit Kat bar," Walt said and headed toward the barn. Colleen moves by his side. Heath brings up the rear. Gillian looks at Lang. Lang nods and heads toward the barn. Bouvier moves toward the house.

"I sense a presence. It is very powerful, but I think it is friendly," Bouvier said, rubbing his pendant.

"Really?" Gillian asked. A friendly spirit is telling you to go into a house filled with poison gas? You may want to rethink that."

Gillian walks off. Bouvier goes up the steps and stares at the door. He looks back and realizes he is alone. Then quickly walks back to the barn.

CHAPTER 12

YOU'RE BAIT

Walt is standing a little ways from the barn. He seems to be deep in thought or even a trance. Collen watches while sipping coffee. Heath drinks coffee while chewing on some jerky. Bouvier comes out and stares at Walt. "What's he doing?"

"At the same thing you should be doing, clearing his mind. We are about to go into battle," Colleen said, emptying her cup on the ground. She looked inside. Lang and Cole both looked annoyed. Gillian was her usual passive self. "I will get the other canisters. You wait for Walt."

"Yes, madam." Health said.

"You call me madam again, and we will have a problem," Collen said, returning to the barn. She went to the packs and spread out the three vests. Then, she put the small leather pouches into the vest pockets. Gillian came over and kneeled down. She started to fill the pockets without being asked. "Thanks."

"What are these?" Gillian asked. "Some kind of weapon I could use?"

"They are like ghost grenades. Supposedly, it will dispel for them a while."

"How long of a while?"

"Depends on how powerful the ghost is."

"So with Echo. We are talking a few seconds." Gillian said, studying the pouch. "Pull the string and throw?"

"Yes."

Gillian puts a few in her jacket pocket. She smiles. "A few seconds can save your life."

"Can I ask you?" Colleen asked. "Why is Lang here?"

"To be honest, I don't know. We were supposed to stay on the chopper. My employer was terrified. I was as surprised as you when he agreed to stay."

"My husband thinks it is about money."

"Men like him. It is always about money. So the white canisters are bigger versions of these?"

"No. The canisters are pure science. They contain a mixture of chemicals Walt and some chemistry guy came up with. The red is our Hail Mary. We set those off. The Echo will be very mad. If things go as bad as we think they will. Get your ass on that tarp."

"Yes, Madam," Gillian says with a smile.

"I will punch you." Colleen pulls on a small knapsack, picks up the vests and the hammer, and walks out. Lang and Coby follow. Walt and Heath are already on the porch holding the axes. She trots over and hands each a vest. "I will get the windows."

"Good," Walt said, putting on the vest and patting the pockets as he watched her go. He nodded at Heath, who already had his vest on. They began to hack at the door hinges. Collen walked around the house, smashing the glass in the windows with the hammer. She pounded the big pieces on the ground until they were almost dust.

"What are they doing?" Bouvier asks.

"Have you ever seen a horror movie?" Gillian said with a smile. Ghosts always seem to lock the doors, trapping the people inside. There are no doors. There is no getting locked in."

"Oh, that can't happen in real life."

"People died up here." She said, looking at the small man. "In very nasty ways. I read the reports."

"And we are looking at the murderer while we waste time with all this mumbo jumbo," Cole said. "We should already been inside, found the bodies, and be on our way home."

"The search party didn't find any more bodies in there. Why would there be bodies in there now? Are you accusing your colleagues of incompetence?" Gillian asked with an amused look.

"Of course not. I am just not comfortable with all this stuff."

Heath's door falls down. He drops his ax and drags the door over to the smothering fire. Colleen walks up as he lays it down. She picks up the can of lighter fluid and sprays it over the door. They look over when Walt's door falls down. The writer seems winded. Heath runs over and helps carry the heavy door over. Colleen sprays more fluid over the doors and pulls out another matchbook. Gillian comes over and snatches. "My turn."

She lights one match. Lights the whole book. Everyone steps back. She tosses on the doors. The door catches fire, sending up a huge fireball. They watch the flames for a second.

Bouvier glances at them and sneaks up to the door. He peeks up and then staggers back. "Oh my God!"

"I won't go in there right now," Walt said, smiling. You know, poison gas."

"What are those?" He stammers, pointing in the house.

Walt looks in. Most of the floor is covered with dead spiders. "Wow, worked."

Walt walks away. Bouvier keeps staring at the spiders. Then, suddenly turned around. "You weren't sure it was going to work?"

"This Echo Hill. You can't be sure of anything. You may want to tune this up." Walt said, tapping the sides of his forehead. "Trust me. You are going to need it."

He stops my Lang. "About a half hour we go in there. There will be no going back. As they say in paranormal circles, that house is a hot spot. People. Probably your daughter has died in there."

"Yet, you and your wife make jokes."

"It's our coping mechanism. There will be no more jokes once we are inside. Let me know if you want me to call the chopper. We still got time."

"Mr. Wilkins, I know a con man when I see one," Lang said. "I don't believe we are in any real danger. All this will help your book sales."

"I am not here to sell books. I am here because you were going to put an innocent man on trial for murder. I haven't figured out why you are here. But you know why I insisted you come."

"Please tell me."

"You're bait. If you really are a direct descendant of Harry Johnson. Echo will be focused on you and not the rest of us. Whoa, did it just get a little colder? Oops, maybe she didn't know that. My bad. Now she does."

CHAPTER 13

INTO ECHO'S DEN

Walt stands in the doorway of Echo's house, holding the shovel. Bouvier peeks over his shoulder. He glances back. "Here we go."

Walt uses the shovel to clear a path through the dead spiders. The others follow in a single file. Bouvier is right behind Walt, fingering his pendant. He keeps moving his face around as if trying to hear something. Colleen comes next but stops to place a red canister on one side of the door and a white one on the other. Lang comes next. Then Gillian. Heath brings up the rear. Stops and looks back at Cole. "You coming?"

"Yes, I was just praying," Cole said, fingering his cross.

"Put a good word in for me."

"Don't trivialize my faith."

"I wasn't. I go to church, too," Heath said and moved forward. I am praying, too. I just don't make a big show of it."

Cole looks down at the dead spiders and shutters and his hand down to his pistol. Only then does he begin to walk.

Colleen stops to toss a red canister on one side and a white one on the other.

Walt has reached the trapdoor and begins to clear an ample space around it. Then, more spiders away from the fireplace. Bouvier comes up and kneels down. He rubs his hand over the trapdoor. "There's not a mark on it. I thought they tried to chop it open."

"They did. They even tried blasting," Collen said, moving past him. Walt had finished clearing a space around the fireplace. He looked at the rack in the fireplace. She pulled off her knapsack and pulled out a red and white canister.

"Careful," Walt said.

She nods. Then, put the canisters around the fireplace.

Walt returns to the trapdoor but notices Cole standing in the middle of the room. "Officer, you may not want to stand there. It's a chandelier with pointy antlers."

Cole looks up and rolls his eyes but moves forward. Walt pushes by Bouvier and runs his hands over the door.

"I have already checked." The psychic said. "It is safe."

"The fact it is freezing doesn't bother you?"

"You said the whole compound is a cold spot. Now I have a suggestion on how to open it."

Walt starts to say something but changes his mind. He looks at Heath and Colleen. They are both holding a small leather pouch. Gillian notices this and pulls one out of her pocket. Walt takes a deep breath and pulls open the door with ease. A nervous laugh comes out of his lips. Then he peeks in. "Alex, you deserved better."

Alex's body is crumpled at the bottom of the ladder. His fingerless hands pressed against his chest. His open eyes are still filled with terror. His mouth is open as if he died screaming.

"Heath, the door," Colleen said.

"Right." Heath moves by the trapdoor and chops off the hinges with his ace. Once this is done. He cares it out and throws it on the fire. After he turns his back and goes back in. The trapdoor slides off the fire and closer to the entrance.

"Okay, let's get him out," Walt said.

"I can't allow that," Cole said, stepping forward. "That tunnel is now a crime scene. We have to protect it."

"Excellent," Walt said, smiling and getting up. "We get to leave. Then you can come back with your crime scene guys and investigate. I thank you, officer."

"We are not leaving without my daughter's body." Lang snarls, stepping in front of the officer. "We are here to find my daughter's body. That is our primary goal. I don't give a damn about your crime scene. You get in my way. I will crush you like the bug you are."

Lang looks back at Walt. "Do we really need to move the body?"

"Well, I think we will be leaving in a hurry. I would rather not climb over a dead body. It is blocking the ladder. If that isn't enough. If we find your daughter's body. We will have to move Alex to get her out."

Cole starts to protest and even puts his hand on his pistol. Gillian looks him in the eye and shakes her head. His hand drops away as he steps back from Lang.

"Move it." Lang snaps.

"This is your party," Walt said, climbing into the tunnel. "Heath, give me a hand."

Heath moves by the trapdoor. Walt manages to push the dead body up high enough for the big man to pull it out. Heath moved it away and respectfully closed her eyes. He bows his head for a moment. Alex's head pops up. "Okay, who is coming?"

"I think it is best I stay here and protect the body," Cole said. Trying to regain some authority. "It is evidence."

"I will take that as no," Alex said. "I know Heath and my wife are coming. I have a feeling you are staying up here, Lang."

"Yes, Gillian and I will stay up here," Lang grumbles.

"Bouvier?" Walt asked, holding up a flashlight and checking to ensure it worked. "Let's do this."

Heath and Colleen climb into the tunnel and click on their flashlights. Walt shines his light down the tunnel. "It looks about the same. It's a dark, creepy tunnel."

They move forward, stopping when Bouvier comes down into the tunnel and stumbles after them. Walt rolls his eyes and then moves forward. They have gone quite a ways down the tunnel when Walt stops. "You bitch."

"What?" Colleen asked, looking past him. There were now two tunnels going off in different directions. "Two tunnels. There was only one last time."

"Yeah, I remember. Echo tried to bury us alive down here." Walt said, moving forward. He leans in the right tunnel and seems to listen. Then moves over to the left and does the same thing. "We go left."

"Wait." Bouvier snaps and pushes ahead. Once again, he rubs his pendent, but this time, he closes his eyes. "No, no, you are wrong. We should go right."

"Listen to me. Echo is playing with your head. She wants to divide us up. Left is the way to go."

"You have mocked and insulted me from the beginning. I tell you, my powers are real. We should go right."

"Please listen to my husband," Colleen pleads. We have been here before. Trust us."

"We go right."

"Bouveir, she is messing with you." Walt sighs.

Heath is leaning against the wall, studying Bouvier. He smiles. "How much did Lang say he would pay you if you found his daughter's body?"

"That has nothing to do with this." Bouvier snaps.

"How much?" Heath said in a harsher tone.

"Five million."

"You are letting your greed..." Walt starts to say.

"I am going right." The psychic snarls and goes down the right tunnel.

"I can't believe he is doing that," Colleen said.

"Maybe he really believes he is a psychic," Heath said. "You tell yourself a lie enough times and begin to believe it."

"Let's go," Walt said, moving into the left tunnel. "I don't understand it. Why hasn't she done anything? She is here. I can feel her."

"Stop trying to figure her out. She's evil and smart. Let's just get this done and go home." Colleen said.

"Your lips to God's ears," Heath said.

They move down the tunnel. Walt stops and frowns. "Where is the skeleton?"

"I don't know, but there is the green glow," Colleen said.

"Yeah, the green glow," Walt said, looking back at Heath. "We're coming to an open chamber. Don't go in."

"Yeah, I will rush into a glowing green chamber." Heath dryly said.

They come to the opening leading into the chamber. Walt stops and looks inside. Audrey Lang is floating over the green crystal. A green light is wrapped around her like a cocoon, and her long hair floats around her face like a halo.

"I really wasn't expecting this," Walt said.

"Is she alive?" Colleen asks, staring at Audrey.

"Alive or dead," Heath said. "She's bait."

CHAPTER 14

NOT SEEING THE LIGHT

Cole is pacing up and down the path created by Walt. He occasionally glances up at the chandelier. "Pointy antlers."

Gillian stands like a statue by the trapdoor. She rubs her hands and sees her breath clouding in front of her. Lang stands off by himself with his arms wrapped around himself. "Sir, I think it is time to go to the circle."

"We're not leaving." Lang snaps, moving closer. "I pay you to protect me and follow my orders."

"That only goes so far, sir," Gillian whispers. "Something is going on here. I can feel it."

"I just feel the cold."

"It's more than that."

Cole had stopped pacing. He pulls out his small bible and begins to thumb through like he is looking for a passage. Without warning, the chandelier comes crashing down. The officer is crushed under the weight of it. Some of the antlers have impaled his body. Blood begins to go out of his mouth as he struggles. Gillian runs over and tries to lift the heavy chandelier. A terrified Lang backs up but stops when his boots bang against the dead spider. Gillian looks back. "HELP ME!"

Lang is frozen with fear. You can see it on his face and in his eyes.

"Great!" Gillian mutters and then notices a greenish fog slowly floating into the house through the windows and entrance. She looks at the door, debating whether she should run, but glances back at the opening on the floor. She pulls out two of the pouches. "Hurry up, you guys."

CHAPTER 15

A VERY WRONG TURN

Bouvier holds up his phone, using it as a flashlight. He is stroking his pendant as he creeps down the tunnel. Sweat is running down his face, and his breath clouds around his face. This tunnel is more crude—a dirt tunnel held up by no visible meanings. The psychic enters a vast cave and stops as green fog covers the floor. He rubs his pendant even harder. "I am protected by the light."

The fog floats up into the air and begins to swirl around. It slowly takes the form of Echo. This time, she is beautiful, with her hair flowing around her body and face. She smiles and moves forward. "Yes, the light does protect you. For I am the light."

"No, you are not!" He stammers, backing up. "You are the darkness. I rebuke you. Go back from where you came!"

"Oh, Aramis, I came from here," Echo said in a lovely voice. She floats closer. A shy smile comes to her lips. "This is my home. "I have always been here and will always remain here. Why do you fear me? I will show you the way to true power. No more tricks. You will have real power."

"NO! NO!" Bouvier stammers, backing up and then stumbling. He falls down. He gasps when the beautiful ghost floats about him. The terrified man holds up his pendant like a cross. "You have no power over me. I am light."

"Tut tut, let's be nice," Echo said, glancing at the pendant. Now, she is almost lying on top of the shivering man. "That is very pretty. I think I will keep that."

"I order you to..." Bouvier starts to say, but Echo grabs his face and kisses him on the lips. He screams into her mouth as the kiss goes on and on.

She finally floats away, holding the pendant. She smiles and dangles it. "Thank you."

Bouvier, now terrified, backs up, sobbing. He manages to get on his hands and knees. As he crawls back down the tunnel, the floor becomes muddy. The psychic struggles in the mud. Mud begins to dribble down from the ceiling. Bouvier manages to get to his feet. He sees the divide and hysterically laughs.

A form erupts out of the ground. It is the dead form of Preston Scott. Rotting with mud and slime running down his face and body. A horrible smile comes to his lips. He grabs Bouvier and pulls him down into the mud. "Come join me!"

"NOOO!" Bouvier screams as he is pulled into the mud. It seems alive as it swirls around him. He manages another scream before being pulled under.

His world becomes blackness and horrible smells. Then, suddenly, he is trapped in a small box of some kind. Bouvier manages to get his flashlight on. The first thing he sees is the bloody scratches on the top of the box. Then, his beam falls on the dead decaying face of Preston. He screams at the realization he has been buried alive.

CHAPTER 15

IT'S ALWAYS SOMETHING

"Okay, here's the plan," Walt said. "Heath, you get behind Audrey and are ready to catch her. Honey, stay here and get ready to throw a couple of pouches. Pray they work. Then get to the entrance and make sure it stays open."

"Good plan. Simple. Basic." Colleen said.

"Let's get this done," Heath said, moving into the chamber. Walt followed but went to the other side. Colleen got two pouches out. Walt studied the floating woman while rubbing his hands together.

"All right, everyone, get ready," Walt said as he put his hands out, palms up. He closed his eyes. His hands began to shake. A small groan came out. The chamber started to shake. The green aura around Audrey began to swirl around. A piercing scream filled the chamber. Audrey flies out and into Heath's arms. "Colleen, now! Heath, get her out of here!"

Heath slings Audrey over his shoulder and rushes out. Walt dives out of the chamber just as Colleen throws two pouches into the chamber. A second later, there is a pop like a small firecracker. A silvery-white cloud fills the chamber. The glowing crystal seems to fade.

Both Walt and Colleen rush out of the chamber. Colleen pushes Heath up the tunnel. She hesitates as she passes where the other tunnel should be, but Walt's yelling makes her move. She reaches the end and scrambles up the ladder.

"What did you find?" Lang asks.

Colleen doesn't answer because she sees Cole's bloody body. Lang's screaming makes her look at him. "We found your daughter. She might be alive."

"She's alive?" Lang looked more annoyed than shocked. He looks around, pulls a small pistol from his back, and hits Colleen on the head. "NOBODY MOVE!"

CHAPTER 16

Walt reaches the tunnel and looks back. Heath comes up with Audrey. There is a green cloud racing down the tunnel toward them. Echo's skeleton comes out of it, screaming like a banshee. Walt throws two pounds. They explode. The ghost vanishes.

"I will go up," Heath yells, climbing the ladder. Hand her up to me!"

Heath climbs out of the tunnel and sees Colleen on the floor, rubbing the back of her head. Lang rushes up. "Don't move!"

"I don't have time for this!" Heath said and punched Lang in the face. Then, he tosses him across the room for good measure. The old man lands in a pile of spiders. He turns as Walt pushes Audrey up. Heath pulls her up and starts her to put down.

"Get her out of here!" Walt yells, climbing out of the tunnel. He throws down two pouches. Then he sees Gillian helping Colleen up. Heath is running out of the house. "Get her out of here!"

Gillian just nods as she helps Colleen toward the door. Walt glances at Lang, kneeling and wiping spider goo off his clothes. He starts to move toward him. Echo explodes out of the tunnel, looking like a hideous green version of herself. Her scream seems to shake the entire house. "I hear you."

Walt runs toward the door, pulling a white fob from his pockets. The ghost expands, filling most of the house. He glances back and dives out the entrance. Walt lands on the porch with a painful groan. He rolls over and presses the fob.

Echo screams as she flies at Walt. The three white canisters suddenly explode, sending a cloud filled with sliver flashes. The ghost is engulfed in the cloud, screams, and returns to the tunnel.

Walt gets up and runs toward the house. Echo's screams fill the air, but he doesn't look back. He dashes into the barn. The others are already on the tarp. Once again, Walt dives and lands inside the tarp.

The horrible green ghost flies up but suddenly stops like she has hit a wall. Her screams and howls fill the barn as she swirls around the tarp, trying to break through.

"Oh, what is happening?" Audrey moans as she sits up and looks up at Heath. "Heath?"

"You all right," Walt asks, kneeling by Colleen.

"Yeah, nothing an Advil won't fix," Colleen said. "And a glass of wine."

"Right there with you?" Gillian asks. "Now what? Where's Lang?"

"Is he crazy or just stupid?" Colleen asks, getting to her feet and watching the ghost swirl around the tarp.

"Dad is here?" Audrey asks. "Don't suppose you anything to eat?"

"Here," Heath said with a smile, handing her Snicker bar.

"Thanks." Audrey takes the candy bar and shakes her head. "In answer to your question. My dad is a little of both."

"Once again," Gillian asked. "Now would be a good time for those Hail Mary red canisters.

"Not yet," Walt said. "Lang is still alive. Let's hope he continues to be stupid."

"Uh-oh," Colleen said as more green ghosts appeared around the tarp. Jerry, Maria, Earl, Wolsky, and Alex are among the dead. "She brought in backup."

Echo and his ghost minions crowd around the tarp, moaning and muttering. "Join us. Be free. Join us."

A silver wall appears, but it shimmers. Walt puts up his hands and closes his eyes. The wall vanishes. "I don't know how long I can hold them back."

CHAPTER 17

ONE LAST SELFISH ACT

Lang stumbles through the dead spiders, kicking them out of the way while wiping goo and spider guts from his face and clothes. He gets to the path and runs to the door. He sees no one and sneaks out. The old man goes to the barn and peeks inside. He shivers at the sight of the ghosts but then smiles. Lang runs past the entrance and out of the compound.

CHAPTER 18

Walt is still holding back the ghosts. The others start throwing the pouches. Some of the ghosts are dispelled. He sees Lang creep by and run off. He waits a few moments and yells, "Echo! The ancestor of Harry Jackson is escaping!"

Echo flies up and looks around. Then flies out of the barn, but the other ghosts stay. Colleen moves beside her husband, pulling out her own fob.

"Not yet!" Walt yells.

Lang runs down the trail, looking frightened but pretty happy with himself. Suddenly, the beautiful Echo appears in front of him. He stumbles to the ground. "Where do you think you are going, ancestor of Harry Jackson!"

"No, that was a lie!" Lang blubbers.

"I can smell his blood in you!" Echo snarls and grabs him by the shirt. She drags back up the trail, past the barn, and into the house. They both go down into the tunnel. The trapdoor flies into the house and slams down on the opening with a loud crash.

"Now!" Walt yells.

Colleen presses the fob. The two canisters explode and fill the barn with a white sparkly cloud. All the ghosts scream and vanish.

"Run!"

The entire group runs out of the barn, with Heath helping Audrey. They leave all their gear, and no one looks back as they escape the compound.

CHAPTER 19

THE HAIL MARY

The group staggers into the logging camp, exhausted. They are panting and sweaty. Heath is holding up Audrey.

"We got to keep moving," Walt said. "She will be back."

"I am already here," Echo snarled, blocking the path. Once again, she was a beautiful woman. "You are all out of tricks."

"Nope, go one more." Walt pants, pulling out his fob and pressing it.

The canisters inside Echo's house explode into massive fireballs. The flames quickly engulf the old wooden house, and a second later, the barn explodes.

"NOOOO!" Echo screams and vanishes.

"MOVE!" MOVE!" Walt yells, pushing down the trail. He glances back and then runs.

Echo flies around the inside of her house, taking in the flames. She screams. A second later, a hard rain came pouring down. The flames begin to die down. The ghost surveys the damage and flies back but bounces into what seems like an invisible wall. "What magic is this?"

Walt leads the group down the trail. They are all being soaked by the pouring rain. He comes into a small clearing. The rain has stopped. Walt looks back and smiles. The others stumble out of the rain. They look up at the blue sky. "This is it. The extent of her power."

"You sure," Gillian asked, still panting.

"Ghosts are always attached to something—something personal. In Echo's case, it's the house and part of the hill." Audrey said, slumping down and pushing back her wet hair. Everyone looked at her. "I know stuff."

"Can I ask why your father was so obsessed with getting you back?" Walt said. "I know it was about money?"

"Money." She nods. "He didn't need me. He needed my body. You see, my dad is like our president. A con man and liar. He is not really a billionaire. His father gave him a ton of money, which he went through. Granddad kept bailing him out. When Granddad died. It turned out he and Grandma had created a trust for me. Which dad couldn't touch? An enormous trust."

"How large?" Colleen asked. "It must be a lot."

"I actually am a billionaire."

"I get it," Gillian said. "He needed your body to prove you were dead, or he would have to wait for seven years to get the money."

"The joke is on him. I have a will he needs to learn about. He doesn't get a cent, but many causes he hates will suddenly be well off."

Suddenly, a camera and headcams fly into the clearing. Echo appears at the edge of the clearing. "You once again escaped. Who helped you?"

"I have no idea what you are talking about," Walt said.

Echo glares at him and snarls, "Don't come back. You may call your flying machine and leave."

She vanishes. Audrey runs over and looks at the gear. "It's all my cameras. Why would she give these back?"

"I guess she wants you to show the world this is a dangerous place."

"Can you call the chopper now?" Audrey asked.

"The only place the chopper can land is back at the logging camp. We would be back on her turf. Trust that bitch. I wasn't born stupid."

Walt takes Colleen's hand. They start down the trail.

Audrey begins to gather up the camera. "A little help."

"I'll carry it," Heath said, taking the cameras and handing another Snicker bar.

"Thanks," She said with a big smile. "I am done with ghosts."

"Me too."

CHAPTER 20

NEW FRIENDS

"So Walt has a sister?" Gillian asks as she reloads her pistol. They are standing in an indoor firing range.

"Yes, older. I never met her." Colleen said, checking her own pistol. "He doesn't talk about her much. Actually, not at all. Apparently, she left or vanished when he was very young."

"Maybe the government took her." Gillian jokes.

"Don't joke. That is one of the reasons Walt keeps his powers secret. Besides, his biggest power is telekinesis. He can't read minds; he just picks up images and emotions. He can't touch stuff and pick up anything. He can't see the future. His powers are useless in helping anyone find a lost one or solve a murder. Heath still dating Audrey?"

"Nice segue into a new topic. Last I heard, they were in France." Gillian said with a smile. "I don't talk about my family either."

The two women take aim and start firing.

CHAPTER 22

WENDY

Walt, dressed in sweat, walks out onto the balcony of his apartment and watches the lights. He smiles.

"You go to Echo Hill again. I will not save your ass."

He turns and looks at shimmering images of a woman dressed in black and heels. She looks like actress Anna Kendrick, with bright red hair and a cute face. "Is this what you look like?"

"Maybe?" She smiles. She turns into the spitting image of Kate Upton in a swimsuit. "Maybe you prefer this?"

"First. Married. Second. I am your brother. So Euuu."

"True." She said, changing back to the Kendrick image. "Now Echo Hill is behind us. You can get back to that book. I really liked the last one."

"Wendy, am I ever going to see you face to face."

"Still too dangerous. But in time. "Sorry about your two friends, Audrey and Heath. I had to blank out their memories of you using your powers. Best to keep that secret."

"Why didn't you do that to Gillian?"

"Oh, she can keep a secret. Besides, Colleen needs a best friend."

"I miss you."

"Me too. Take care of yourself, bro," she said as the image faded. I will always have your back unless you go back to Echo Hill. Then all bets are off."

Then she is gone.

Wendy does look like the actress, except she is taller and has blonde hair. The young woman is dressed in black slacks and a red turtleneck. She is standing on top of a building, looking down at Walt. She smiles, but then the smile vanishes.

Two men in black suits wearing fedoras climb out of a black sedan. They look around.

"Oh god, you guys have to update your wardrobe," Wendy said with a shake of her head, who was standing behind them. "Who wears fedoras anymore? The guys in the movies are much cooler."

The two men whirl around, pulling out strange pistols. They have wood hands with long silver barrels. They both freeze in place.

"The psychic blocker is almost there," Wendy said, approaching the men. I can still hear your heartbeat, and your partner breathes like a wounded rhino. I don't know what a wounded rhino sounds like, but it is fun to say. This is new?"

Wendy takes the pistol out of the man's hand and studies it. Then looks into the man's face. "So what does it do? Sonic Blaster? That is kind of a comic book name for a weapon."

She points the weapon at their car and pulls the trigger. A loud thump comes out. Then, car windows explode, and the roof and tires are flattened. "Wow, so cool. My sister-in-law and her new bestie would love these."

Wendy walks over and takes the other pistol. She walks away and turns. "I will just hang on to these. I told you to stay away from my bro. What part of that don't you understand?"

She points both pistols and fires. Both fly men to the end of the street, landing with a sickening, crushing sound. Wendy strolls and looks at the dead men. The bodies look like every bone in their bodies is broken. Wendy looks at the guns. "I just meant to stun. My bad."

Wendy walks up the street to a cherry red 1969 Camaro in excellent condition. She slips into the car and smiles.

"Great car."

Wendy looks over at a teenager standing on the curb. "Yes, it is. The best part is that it does not have a computer or electronics—just a lot of horsepower."

The teenager watches her start the car and rev it a few times. It races up the street. He pulls out his phone but stops when the Camaro backs up and stops. "Did you really think you fooled me? Silly boy."

Wendy aims one of the pistols at the teenager.